# A DEAD MARKET

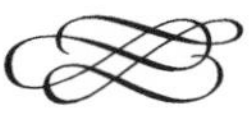

CEECEE JAMES

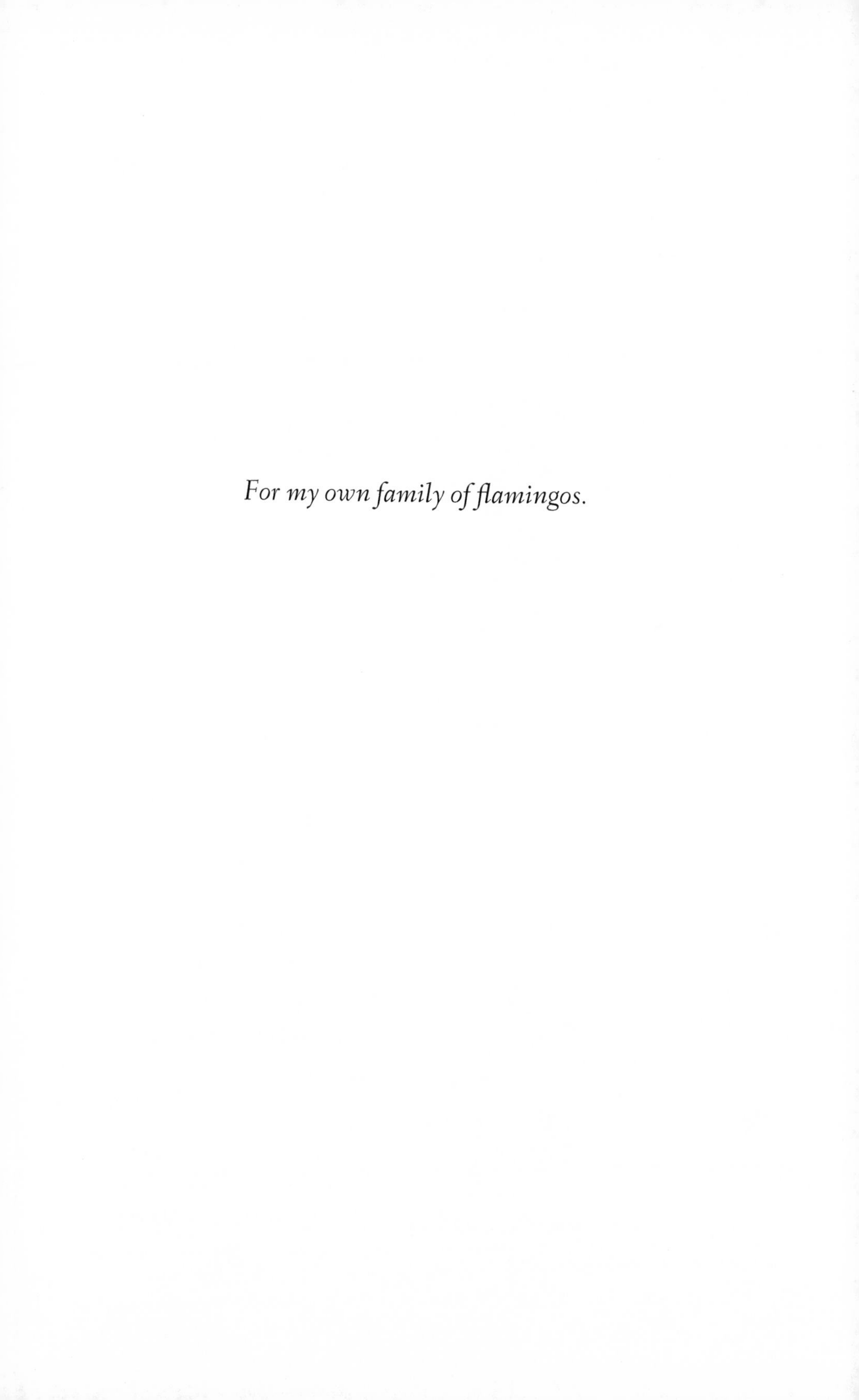

*For my own family of flamingos.*

# CONTENTS

# INTRODUCTION

Stella O'Neil finally has her first listing! A cute cabin with a gorgeous lake on eighty acres of breathtaking land. There's just one tiny problem: the body floating in the lake.

If that weren't unsettling enough, her phone rings off the hook with hundreds of potential buyers. In fact, the property is overrun with them! Stella digs out the truth that the lake is the obscure clue in an old legend that has been solved on the Internet.

But only if her troubles stopped there. She runs into one buyer who won't take no for an answer. He seems to have way too much personal information about Stella herself, but the police refuse to take him seriously. As things continue to develop, she is certain that she being hunted by someone with some sort of grudge against her.

Stella has to solve the murder and figure out the riddle so she can untangle herself from this legal and personal mess... before things go too far.

# CHAPTER 1

Sunlight splintered across the floor, reflecting off the shards of a glass fruit bowl that I'd just dropped. I stared at it guiltily, afraid to meet my grandfather's eyes. After all, we'd just met a few weeks prior. Now, like the proverbial bull in a china shop, I'd broken his deceased wife's cherished heirloom.

I heard a raspy sound, like wind over dead leaves, and glanced up to see he was laughing. The reaction was so unexpected, I hardly knew what to do next.

"You should see your face," he wheezed.

I bristled at that. "I feel terrible! What do you mean I should see my face?"

His eyes twinkled behind his coke-bottle thick glasses. "Stella,

I can tell you're sorry. Don't worry. This wasn't one of your grandma's favorites."

"It wasn't?" I asked.

"No. This came from the neighbor when she brought me some pears last year. Nicest lady ever." He tottered over and pointed out the window, his finger as knobby as the apple tree branch outside.

I followed his gesture and saw a huge house on the other side of the hedge. Cars and a van filled the driveway.

"That's the Baker Street bed-and-breakfast," Oscar said. His name was Oscar, and that's what he asked me to call him, so that's what I did. He had the body of a man who had once been fit, but long years and a hard life now curved his spine and shortened his height. He stared at me, his eyes blinking behind his black-framed lenses. "The owner's name is Cecelia," he continued. "She's my new cutie."

"Your new cutie, huh?" I said as I got a broom. Oscar's Pomeranian came prancing over. I shooed her away so she wouldn't step on the glass and made quick work of sweeping up the broken bowl. It took me a minute to remember where he kept the trash.

"Pantry," he said dryly.

Yes, that's right. I located the plastic can and tossed the chunks of glass.

After returning the broom and pan, I sat down at the table across from Oscar. It was set with two mugs and a plate of cinnamon toast. Sensing the coast was clear, the little dog came running back.

"Come on, Peanut," I said, patting my lap.

Oscar harrumphed loudly.

I quickly corrected myself. "I mean Bear. Come on, Bear."

Bear was the name Oscar called her now, but Peanut was the animal's original name. Oscar detested that name—it's sissified, he said—so it came down to a battle of the wills. I can tell you who was coming ahead. Normally, the dog didn't answer to anything but Peanut, but today, the dog jumped up regardless. She spun around twice in my lap. Her sharp nails dug into my leg until she finally found a sweet spot and settled down.

"So you have plans later on, do you?" he asked before crunching on toast.

I nodded, stroking the dog's silky fur on her neck. "I have a house showing in about an hour." I took a sip of coffee and then confessed, "It's the first time I've done it by myself. I'm nervous."

"Pshaw," Oscar waved his hand, scattering crumbs of sugar. "It will be as easy as drinking a glass of water. You'll see."

I stared at my mug, highly doubting that. It hadn't helped that I'd walked in on my uncle, who was also my boss and the owner of Flamingo Realty, talking with Kari, someone who had trained me and I also considered a friend. I wrinkled my nose as the memory played in my mind.

I'd heard them as I approached his office. When I walked in, Uncle Chris and Kari both looked guilty, like a dog caught eating from the butter container.

"Stella, how are you?" my uncle had said, trying to recover his composure.

I'd been blunt and to the point. "I heard you guys."

They exchanged looks.

"Heard us what, hun?" Uncle Chris said, smiling like when I was five and had tried to tell him about a dream I'd had. It had been annoying then, and was annoying now.

"Heard you say you didn't think I was cut out to sell real estate." I crossed my arms, raised an eyebrow, and gave them the stare-down.

Uncle Chris had cleared his throat as Kari jumped in. "He didn't mean it the way it sounded. I mean, my first few sales were so sloppy."

Sloppy was not my favorite adjective when it referred to me, but I'd known instantly what she'd meant. I'd just signed my first contract with the seller. Unfortunately, I'd accidentally left off half the signatures. I'd also let them talk me down a full half a point on my commission. So far, my first two official days as an agent had been running back and forth to fix that mistake.

"Sorry. I'm sure you'll develop the killer instinct." Uncle Chris clapped me on the back.

Remembering that now, I sighed again.

"What are you huffing over there for?" Oscar asked. "You sound like an air compressor filling a tire."

"Uncle Chris doesn't have a lot of faith in me," I said, and then immediately felt guilty. Chris and my dad, Steve, were Oscar's sons. Neither of them would have anything to do with their dad.

"How are my sons doing, anyway?" Oscar asked.

I shrugged. "Being as stubborn as usual." I smiled.

"Yeah, well, I wouldn't know," Oscar said, hinting at the feud.

I wanted to remind him that he hadn't exactly reached out to them either, but I didn't want to deal with the grumpy response. Instead, I set the dog on the floor where she promptly ran over and jumped on Oscar's lap. I grabbed my mug and brought it to the sink. As I was rinsing it, the alarm chimed on my phone, reminding me of my appointment to meet the potential buyers.

"All right, I guess that means showtime. Thanks for breakfast." I shrugged back into my sweater. It was cool this early fall morning.

"Where's it at again?" Oscar asked.

"It's at Johnson Lake."

Oscar's bushy eyebrows rose above his thick eyeglass frames. "You mean the one that flooded?"

"I'd heard something about the original homestead flooding. That was years ago, though right? Like ancient history?"

"Ancient history that everyone knows! What is it with today's generation not realizing the importance of knowing history?"

I bit my tongue. "What was so important about it? It was just a dam being built, right?"

"It was more than that. It has to do with a property line squabble that went back over a hundred years. Still going on, last I heard. I'm wondering what's going to happen when you sell the place?"

"You mean the neighbors? Why didn't they get it surveyed?"

"Oh, they have, but the lines have been blurred so many times that neither would accept the surveyor's results. I even heard the neighbor has shipping containers that cross the property line. He keeps them way down deep in the woods."

I worked my keys out from my purse. "Well, I guess I'll cross that bridge when I come to it."

Oscar stared hard at me with a shake of his head. "You'll see. You'll see."

"Ha!" I laughed. "After dealing with the men in *this* family, I think I'm more than prepared to tackle another feuding challenge."

"Do you hear that, Bear? She thinks her family is as sweet as a cake of burnt corn bread." Oscar whispered to the dog. At least, I assumed he thought he was whispering. It came out with the subtlety of a chainsaw.

"I'm just saying I have lots of experience with stubborn men who like to argue." I balked then. Had I gone too far?

There was that raspy leaves sound again.

Oscar was laughing.

# CHAPTER 2

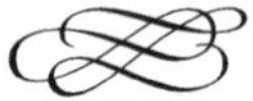

The road to the Johnson Lake curved through the beautiful land of the Appalachian Mountains. The autumn colors of the trees took my breath away. Blood red, fiery orange, and yellow the shade of lemons.

It reminded me of the first time I'd seen my dad cry.

I don't remember much of my mom, but I remember the day she left. It's one of those memories that will stay with me until the day I die, but not for the reasons you might think.

I remember it was sunny. My dad stood in front of the opened front door with his hand on the frame. I saw his back, the light shining around him, and the edges of his silhouette seemed to glow. It must have been autumn because I remember the light dancing in the distance in the leaves of red, yellow, and orange.

It was silent, a silence that no words could fill. I now recognized it as the moment when the painful reality of losing my mother made its first presence known as a black hole in our lives. A loss I never understood, but whose gapping emptiness stole from every memory and experience from then on, always whispering what could have been.

After a moment, my dad's head dropped. His knuckles rose white under the skin as his trembling fingers clenched the wood, as if the weight of what our new life would be like, always dancing around the black hole, fell on his shoulders. And then, slowly, he shut the door.

He turned around and saw me. Whispered my name. I was very young, at the age where I thought fireflies were fairy warriors who battled the darkness to protect the sleeping flowers.

I ran over on legs still chubby and clumsy. He reached for my hand, squeezing it as if to reassure himself that I was really there. And then he stooped down to lift me into his arms. He hugged me tight and I felt his chest heave.

I caught his cheeks between my two hands, hands pale against his tan skin—his face scratchy to my palms.

"Hi, Sweet Pea," he whispered. His eyes were red-rimmed.

"You ready for breakfast?" His face lied about breakfast, with its promises that everything was okay. It contorted as he grimaced to control himself, his breaths coming in gulps.

I remember gazing into his eyes, my little heart filled with worry. I realize now that I was looking into the eyes of a man who was heartbroken. Who knew he couldn't protect me from the pain that was to come.

I didn't say anything, just stared. A tear trickled down the side of his nose. I watched it with wonder.

"Daddy, are you hurt?" I asked. Can daddies get hurt?

He squeezed his lips together—his eyes—and he nodded.

Fear filled my little body. I hugged him, like I could give him my strength. "Don't worry, Daddy. I'll get you a band-aid."

He carried me over to the couch where he lay down on his side. I sat in the tiny space left and patted his shoulder as he curled around me. He hid his face in my arm, his breath warm gusts against my skin.

I made it my goal right then, to always take care of him. I would be his firefly against the dark. With my finger, I drew a row of smilie faces down his arm.

Finally, he sighed. His eyes were wet when he looked at me, but his lip lifted at the corner, which made me feel better. "I'm okay, Sweet Pea. We'll be okay. I'll make sure of it."

And then I remember that Dad had slowly stood up and wandered into the kitchen to make some cinnamon toast for me.

Just like Oscar had done.

They'd both done their best as fathers. I knew that. Everyone needed their father, and I think my dad needed his. I was determined to bring them back together.

Sighing as the memory faded to its last painful squeeze, I flipped on the blinker and turned down a dirt road that led into a valley. It was beautiful back here, a land nearly untouched by human hands. If you ignored the power lines, that is. The road eased to the left and opened up, and the explanation for the flooded fields became obvious. The acreage sloped to a large lake that could be seen in the distance cuddling the bottom of the valley. Underneath all that water was where the original house had once had been.

An old barbed wire fence filled with half-dead blackberries seemed to race along side me. I eased off the gas to watch for a driveway opening. Finally, I found it and pulled to the side of the road. I searched the length of the fence as I climbed out. Now, where was that property corner? There was nothing that stood out.

What should have been standing out though, was the Flamingo Realty's mascot. Yesterday, I'd made a quick stop to hang the for-sale sign and plunk down the four-foot plastic pink flamingo. But now he was missing.

I walked along the road to see if it had blown down. Sure enough, there it was in the bottom of the ditch. Grumbling about the blackberries, I carefully climbed down and yanked it out.

The plastic bird was unwieldy. I waddled back with it and jammed it hard into the ground next to the post.

There.

Not quite satisfied, I gave the bird a little jerk to level it, and then got back in the car to pull it into the driveway.

After parking, I slammed the car door shut and straightened my sweater as I surveyed the property. This place was a steal. Someone was going to really love it.

Oh shoot, I'd forgotten to hang my sign, the one with my name on it. It was so shiny and official. I'd been nearly giddy when I'd received it this morning. But then overhearing Uncle Chris and Kari sort of flushed that down the toilet. *You know what? I'm going to prove them wrong.*

I walked back to the post and hung it up, then stood back to admire it. Stella O'Neil. A smile spread across my face, and I tapped it lightly, sending it swinging. Still smiling, I straightened the flamingo one more time.

It was funny that the bird was a trademark of my uncle's company. Anyone would have thought the flamingo was the antithesis of his personality—him being this burly, retired bad-boy, race car driver with a reputation of being a hot head.

But just one lost bet in a high-stakes car race led him to this.

A breeze lifted the hair off of my neck. I sniffed deeply. Fresh. Clean.

Cold.

I shivered and buttoned up my sweater, then crossed my arms. Definitely should have worn something a little warmer for today.

It was easy to see why the wind picked up here. Glaciers had once scraped through this valley, creating a perfect channel for the breezy air.

And water. I walked to the edge of the driveway where it met the lawn. Eighty acres was a lot of land.

After I'd left Oscar's house, I'd made a quick phone call to Kari for a little more information. She'd grown up around here and I figured she'd know the scoop.

The story she told me was that, years ago, Brookfield diverted the river to prevent the yearly flooding they dealt with. The Johnson's, the original owners, had been given notice to move their things, but something must have become screwed up, because the house, along with everything they owned, had been buried under millions of gallons of water. Their furniture, clothing, dishes, the whole shebang. Gone.

They'd tried to save what they could but there wasn't much salvageable. Even more gruesome, the original Mr. Johnson died on one of those dives.

Kari whispered that the gossip in these parts was that the neighbor had drowned him in revenge for an old property line dispute in which his cow was killed, and now the Johnson ghost wandered the land.

Well, from that point on, everyone stayed away. The Johnson family moved to town and the property exchanged hands with another family member who sold it again.

And then a single man drove down from Pittsburgh and offered the family a ridiculously low amount, but the family had taken it. That man had built a house, this little one that I was standing before right now.

You would never know the history, seeing the property now. Everywhere I looked, the terrain had that softened appearance that autumn inching into winter brought. Even the lake was peaceful, with a few weeping willows along the grassy shores.

Now that I knew more about the property, I was hoping the reputation about the ghost had died long ago. When I'd written the realty listing, I'd tweaked the verbiage to describe it as 'an artist's get-away for someone to build their dream house.' Hopefully, these potential buyers I was meeting were as much in the dark as I had been about this place.

I walked toward the quaint little house built far from the original homestead, new by Brookfield gossip standards, but my listing papers said it had been there since 1980. It had white shutters and rickrack around the awnings. Although just shy of nine-hundred-square feet, the home had a charm that reminded me of a gingerbread house. All it needed were a few peppermint candies on the front wall.

My phone rang, and I answered it, wondering if it was the buyers. "Hello?"

"Stella, darling. How are you?" a woman asked. I recognized her right away. It was Mrs. Crawford, my landlord. She was in her seventies, and as graceful and lovely as any legendary movie star.

"I'm great. Standing in front of my first listing, actually. I'm supposed to be meeting people here, any minute."

"Oh, how fun. What house is it? Any I know of?"

"I'm at the Johnson's house. The one with the lake." I figured if Oscar knew about it, then she did as well.

"I know of it. Good luck with that, honey. You know what they say...."

"What do they say?" I smiled, expecting to hear the flood story again.

"That there's a treasure buried at the bottom of that lake."

"What? Are you serious?" Hearing some old wives' tale was the last thing I expected her, of all people, to say. She was a sensible, well-traveled woman.

"Yes. I remember it well. They talked about it when I was in school, you know. Kids dared each other to go in the water. Supposedly there was a root cellar with a fortune hidden inside."

"A fortune? Really?"

"Well, who knows. The treasure was never truly discussed. We all had our own imaginations on what it could be. I, of course, always fancied it was a great chest filled with gold. It wasn't that hard to believe. You know, there were decades where people didn't put any trust in banks. Back then, after horses or crops were sold, they'd stash their money in mattresses even. Who knew what the treasure was."

"You think the money's still there?"

"Oh, surely not. Any paper money would have rotted away by now. And I've found treasure chests filled with gold pieces are decidedly rarer than the cartoons that I grew up with led me to believe."

"Yeah, that and quicksand."

She chuckled. "I guess every town has a story about an old house. This one even has a ghost. Old Mr. Johnson."

I glanced at the water and shivered and paced to the other end of the porch. "Don't remind me. I'm here alone at the moment."

"It's supposed to walk along the shore of the lake every night. Of course, it's all just a rumor. You know how we like to have our spooky tales out here. Now, let me get to the reason I called. I have someone I'd like you to meet."

"Okay." That oh-no feeling prickled down my spine. I knew exactly where this conversation was going. You couldn't be in your late twenties without having people trying to constantly set you up with someone they knew would be *perfect* for you.

"He's a friend of mine. I'm having a dinner party in a few days. Would you like to come?"

"Dinner?" Drat. She was being tricky, not giving me an exact day where I could beg off by saying I was busy. I tried to sneak the time out of her. "What night is it again?"

"I have a few options. I want to make sure you can make it."

I closed my eyes. This was getting worse and worse. "That's so nice, but I don't want to inconvenience you. I have so much on my plate with this sale. I have to be available at a moments notice."

"Nonsense. You've been hiding away out in that little house of mine like a hermit crab in its shell. It's time to get out and meet people." She paused and then added, "You can't hide forever."

I swallowed hard. She was the only one, out of my dad, my uncle, and my new friend, Kari, that had an inkling on why I'd moved from Seattle to Pennsylvania. It was just too close for comfort. "Okay, well I guess I can try to be there. What night again?"

"How about Tuesday? Can you make it that night?"

Let's see. My evening plans that night included finishing my laundry and maybe tackling the grunge in my bathtub. I was also planning to try my new charcoal mask.

In other words, not busy.

"Yeah, I can make it." I couldn't keep the dread out of my tone.

She laughed. "I'm looking forward to it. Come with an open mind. David is quite an interesting fellow. I'm sure you will both have a lot to talk about."

I tried not to groan. Talking to a man was the last thing I wanted to do at this time of my life. I paced down the side of the house and into the sunshine in the backyard. The sun's rays warmed my skin as I gazed at the lake again.

"Sounds lovely." I sighed.

"I'm planning on a light fair. Maybe some chicken fricassee."

I tuned her out as I stared at the bright ripples on the lake.

What was *that* out in the water?

One second later, I was screaming.

# CHAPTER 3

The screams poured out of me, something a little shy of coherent words, more like long shrieks.

"Stella!" Mrs. Crawford's firm voice was meant to snap me out of my shock. "Stella, answer me this minute. What's going on?"

"Call 911!" I finally managed to gasp out.

"Stella! Tell me what's happened!"

By now, I was racing down to the lake's side. There was a body out in the water, floating with its arms and legs spread wide like a starfish. When I'd first seen it, I'd thought it was a black trash bag. It wasn't until I saw the silver air tank on the body's back that I realized it was a diver.

"There might still be time!" I yelled. "There's a body in the water! Please call for help."

"You've got it," Mrs. Crawford said and immediately hung up. I dropped the phone in my purse and started sloshing out into the water.

"Hey!" I yelled. "Hey, buddy!"

There was no response. The body joggled with the waves, looking like a fishing bobber tossed from a boat. I waded out to my knees, and then to my thighs. The body floated up and down, moving farther away. Other than that, there was no other movement.

As it drifted toward the center of the lake, I realized there was nothing more I could do. I wasn't a strong swimmer. I never had been. People used to call me arm-floaties back in junior high summer camp because I wouldn't go in the water without a life jacket. Seeing where the body was now, I didn't think I could make it all the way there, let alone bring the person back with me.

I splashed back over to the bank and sat on the grass. I could barely breathe under the weight of helplessness.

Fortunately, I wasn't alone for long. Soon, wailing sirens heralded the long chain of police cars and ambulances that raced up the road. I walked up the hill to meet the emergency vehicle parade turning into the driveway.

The first officer to approach me introduced himself as Officer Taylor. He took a quick statement while the other cops pulled out an inflatable boat and immediately set it up. Within minutes, two of the officers were in the boat, paddling to the center of the lake.

I crossed my arms and shivered, soaking wet from my waist down. A blanket draped over my shoulders, and I glanced up and smiled gratefully at the paramedic.

When the police reached the body, one of them dragged it close and pulled off the diver's mask. I could see the officer shake his head, and then heard the mic from the cop next to me squawk. A code was given. As soon as that code was received, the heightened sense of urgency dissipated immediately. It didn't take rocket science to understand that the diver was indeed, truly dead.

I turned away from the shore, feeling like I might throw up. Officer Tayler approached me again with a few more questions, and then I was left alone.

I couldn't believe what had just happened. Waves of surrealness washed over me. How long had he been there? Had it just occurred?

At the sound of tires in the gravel, I turned to see a black car pull up. A man in a sports jacket climbed out and briskly walked over to join the group of police.

"Who is he?" I asked the officer closest to me.

He glanced in that direction. "That's the coroner."

"Why the yellow tape?" I asked. I was confused to see two officers stringing it at the end of the driveway, actually attaching the first end to my sign. The remaining end they fastened to the mailbox on the other side of the driveway. Oddly enough, the mailman was there, trying to put in a flyer. I dumbly wondered who would collect it now.

"We always do it for a murder." The cop said the words bluntly.

My jaw dropped. It felt like the ground shifted under my feet and I nearly fell over. I grabbed the cop's elbow for balance. He glanced at my hand with eyebrows raised and gently extricated himself.

"It's a murder?" I whispered.

"Yeah." He nodded. Then he made a slashing motion to his neck. "Someone got the body with a knife."

Oh boy. Why did he tell me that? I reeled for a second at the visual, finally sitting on the ground with a flop. *Look at the pretty stars.*

He squatted next to me, his boots squeaking. "You okay? Need me to have medical come look at you?" He fanned his notebook over my face.

I was breathing fast. My cheeks felt hot, the rest of me cold. I cupped my hands over my mouth to try to slow my hyperventilating down.

A man had been murdered and in a gruesome way.

The stretcher rattled past on its way down to the lake and brought me another chilling shiver.

"So you didn't see anything, then?" the officer asked. I shook my head and squeezed my eyes closed.

"No cars, no one running in the woods, no one in the house?" he prompted.

"No. I didn't see anyone," I answered.

"And what were you doing out here, again?"

I pointed limply to the signpost. "Hanging the sign. I was supposed to meet a client."

"Did he ever show up?"

I shook my head and then shrugged. "He might have and then been scared away by all of this." I vaguely waved in the direction of the emergency personnel milling about their vehicles.

He studied the flamingo, enrobed with the yellow tape flapping in the breeze. His eyebrow arched, and he wrote some more.

"You going to be sticking around town?" he asked, still scribbling.

Wait, what was this? Was I a suspect? "Yes. Of course I am."

He nodded and stood up. A second later another swarm of officers swept by, heading down to the shore of the lake.

I heard what sounded like the hundredth car drive up. Was this finally my clients? I wearily rose to my feet to see.

It was Uncle Chris. He parked his sports car and climbed out, the sunshine glinting brightly off the polished chrome of his Jaguar. He searched around, and I waved. Seeing me, he marched over with determined steps.

An officer stopped him. Uncle Chris said a few words and pointed to me. The officer let him pass.

Uncle Chris was breathing heavily by the time he reached the house. He wiped his face with his palm. "Day's warmed up," he said and unbuttoned his winter coat. Then he looked at me. "You okay?"

I nodded. "He was murdered," I whispered, wrapping the blanket more securely around me. Standing there, with my pants clinging to my legs and shoes squelching, I felt like a cat that had been dragged out of a fish tank.

Uncle Chris stared down at the lake. I followed his gaze for a second, just in time to see them hoist the body up on a gurney with a thump. Nausea quaked through me, and I turned away to count the beech trees as a distraction.

"They tell me it was Old Man Lenny," Uncle Chris noted. He reached into his front pocket and slid out a cigar. His teeth nipped off the tip and then he lit it with a few puffs. The coal glowed bloody red. He exhaled a dark plume of smoke.

"Who?" I asked. The scent of the cigar was a welcome distraction.

"The guy who... met his maker," he said as if he were trying to soften the verbiage.

It didn't work, but I appreciated the effort. "The officer was asking me if I'd seen anyone here."

"You're lucky, girl. If you had come here a little earlier...." He let that thought hang in the air without finishing it.

Holy cow. He was right! What if I had come earlier and seen a struggle? Or had been identified by the murderer? Would I be floating out in that lake myself?

I shuddered and wrapped the blanket tighter.

"It's no joke," he said again. "Someone up there's watching out for you. You're a lucky girl."

I nodded. "So, Old Man Lenny...who is he exactly?"

"Lenny Johnson. He's the one who sold the seller the property in the first place. In fact, that's his grandpa's place under the water down there."

"Why was he here? And who would kill him?" I shielded my eyes from the sun and stared down at the lake again. A paramedic was zipping the body bag. But what was the other officer carrying?

"What is that?" I asked, at the same time as my uncle.

"That's an air tank, is it?" Uncle Chris added, answering himself.

That's right. I had seen it earlier. The clunky heavy thing looked straight out of a World War Two movie. Water dripped from its cylinder sides as the officer heaved it up on his shoulder.

"I guess Lenny was hunting for something," Uncle Chris said.

"There was more than one person hunting," I amended.

He nodded and took another drag off his stogie. "You're right. There must have been at least two people. And my guess is that one of them found what they were looking for."

I nodded. But, what could they have found in that old cabin under the water that would be worth the death of another? A real treasure chest? And why were they searching *now*, especially after all these years? Why not sooner?

An officer walked past us.

"Excuse me." Uncle Chris stopped him. He gestured with his cigar toward the gurney bumping up the side of the hill. "Any idea how Lenny died?"

The officer shook his head. "I have nothing to say other than he still needs to be identified."

Uncle Chris arched an eyebrow. "Come on, now. You know who it is. Heck, I know who it is. You're not going to say?"

The cop's face turned red. I was surprised to see he was angry. "Listen, you might think you're some hot shot storming into our town and selling all our property to be built into apartment buildings, but that's not the way it works around here. We don't tell anyone but the next of kin who it is. If and when the public needs to know, the Sheriff will hold a press conference. Got it?"

Uncle Chris gave a slow nod, seemingly unimpressed by the officer's sharp tone. He puffed his cigar and squinted some more. I remembered how his old comrades used to be some questionable characters in the past, so I could understand his lack of fear. I personally was shocked by the officer's accusation and was glad to have my uncle by my side.

"I don't know what his problem is," I whispered to Uncle Chris. "The first cop I talked to was nicer."

The stretcher wheeled past us, its wheels squeaking as they ground over the dirt. A clump of grass caught in one of the wheels and the body shuddered as the stretcher jerked to a stop. After clearing the debris, the paramedics continued on to the ambulance.

"Well, that's interesting," Uncle Chris mused as they moved past us.

"What's interesting?" I asked.

"The tank. It had a gull sticker slapped on it."

"Yeah?" I said, all ears.

"There's only one place I know of that has stickers like that."

"Where's that?"

"Laughing Gull Sport Shop." He jabbed his cigar in the direction of the barbed wire fence. "The business of the not-so-friendly feuding neighbor over there."

# CHAPTER 4

We waited around another twenty minutes or so, and then we were cleared by the police to leave. Uncle Chris suggested I go home and relax, which sounded like a great idea to me. It was only after I'd driven half-way home that I realized my buyers had never shown up for their appointment. I suspected my original assumption was correct in that the police cars and ambulance scared them off.

My stomach growled. After missing lunch, I needed some comfort food so I stopped off at the grocery store in Brookfield to pick up some ingredients for my favorite meal—spaghetti with meat sauce.

The store was crowded, as was to be expected near dinner time, and I was bummed to find all of the carts gone. I walked inside and searched for the hand-held baskets, spying a stack next to the customer service desk.

A woman was talking to the clerk manning the Lotto counter. As I reached for a basket, I heard the customer say, "Did you hear about the murdered guy they pulled out of Johnson Lake?"

I nearly fell over. Now, I'd heard news traveled fast in a small town, but this was insane.

"I sure did," the clerk answered, chomping on a piece of gum. "They say it was Old Man Lenny."

"No!" exclaimed the first. She then asked for two packs of cigarettes.

I spun around and grabbed a magazine. Nonchalantly, I flipped to the middle, trying to look as absorbed as possible in the article. *Definitely not eavesdropping on you, ladies.*

"Yep. They say he was searching for his family's buried treasure." The clerk set the packs on the counter.

"You think it's still there after all this time?" the woman asked, sounding skeptical.

"I remember when my brothers used to dive in that water. If anyone could have found it, those two sure would have."

They laughed and the customer plopped her wallet on the

counter. "I know that neighbor, Roy Merlock, is a nasty piece of work."

Slowly I eased around a circular rack of DVD's, head down. Wow, this magazine article was *so* interesting.

"He's always been that way. I went to school with his daughter. She was as stuck up as the days are long." The clerk leaned against the counter.

"What about that new guy? I don't trust him. And he was out there first thing this morning. Discovered the body even! Pretty suspicious, if you ask me."

"What new guy?" the clerk asked, processing her card.

"You know, the one who owns that cheesy realty."

My heart sputtered in my chest. They were talking about us!

"Can't stand that man. They should definitely investigate him. Who knows, this could all be some sick publicity stunt, trying to drum up interest for the sale of the property." The clerk bagged the items.

"Wish they'd get out of our town. All he does is bring in developers."

"Heck, get out of our state even! Go back to California!"

"Is that where he's from?" asked the customer.

"Probably. It seems our entire state is filled with them. Just what we need around here. Some more McMansions," the clerk answered, snapping the gum in her mouth.

Sweat gathered in my armpits and my face flushed. My uncle had every right to be in Brookfield as they did.

Oh, boy. I just caught myself staring at them. Glaring, most likely. I stuffed the magazine back and walked away.

I hated how the Flamingo Realty was being treated. My jaw clenched. People wanted to move. Well, realtors were awfully helpful in making that happen.

The aisles had dissolved into a crowded obstacle course of grocery carts and little kids as I stomped my way through. I swept a package of spaghetti noodles into my basket and then found the sauce. The whole time I was thinking of what I would have *liked* to have said to the clerk.

Finally, I grabbed my phone and called Kari. I needed to vent.

"Are you in the middle of something?" I asked when she answered.

"Just cleaning the house. I was about to do the toilets, so you saved me. What's going on?"

"I'll make this quick. Did you hear what happened out at Johnson Lake?"

She hadn't, having been doing laundry with the music blasting all morning, so I quickly filled her in.

Her next words sounded as high and excited as a pig's squeal running from wrestlers at a rodeo. "Are you serious? Next time call! Like right away!"

I snickered and turned one of the soup cans so I could read the label. "They say it was Lenny. Do you know who that is?" I couldn't bring myself to use the name Old Man before the Lenny, especially since I hadn't known him.

"Aww, poor guy. Yeah, I do. It was his grandpa's place under the water down there."

"I heard. Can you believe someone killed him?" I glanced around, realizing I'd said that with my loud phone voice. A mother glared at me before grabbing her preschooler's hand and hurrying out of the aisle.

"I'm shocked. He was the nicest guy ever," Kari's voice faded at the last word as she went deep in thought.

"You actually knew him?" I asked, quieter this time.

"Yeah, I knew him. Everyone knew him. He worked at the White Rangers restaurant. Have you ever been there?"

"No. I really haven't been anywhere yet," I admitted. "I'm kind of an introvert." I was more of a fast food connoisseur anyway, if I did eat out.

"Oh, girl, we have to cure you of that," she chided.

I wasn't so sure I wanted to be cured, but I held my tongue.

"Anyway," she continued. "The restaurant is out on Hobble Road. It's an amazing place. They have an actual horse arena inside."

"Inside the restaurant?" I wandered through the store, looking for the meat section.

"Well, the restaurant is on the second floor and overlooks the arena. They prance out on their horses and do shows. It's pretty amazing. You should go, sometime. And Old Man Lenny was the chef. He was famous for his food too." She thought for a second. "I suppose Mike is going to be the chef there now."

"Who's Mike?"

"He's been the prep cook for a long time. There was a little gossip that they'd both wanted to be the chef. They had a bit of a squabble over it, and of course, Old Man Lenny won."

"Hmm. And what about the customers there? Do you think any of them could have wanted him dead? Maybe someone thought he'd poisoned them?" I was shooting in the dark. But, the guy was murdered. *Someone* had to have done it.

She paused. "I suppose anything's possible, but he was such a down-to-earth nice guy. Like an old cowboy. He always accommodated my kid's allergies without batting an eye and even gave them extra large servings of fries."

"So, no enemies, huh?" I'd reached the meat cooler of the store by now and added a package of hamburger to my basket.

She was quick to answer back, "You're right. There was one guy who couldn't stand him. The Johnson's old neighbor. Even after the Johnson's moved, their feud was pretty well known. But everyone was on the Johnson's side. No one can stand Roy Merlock."

"Well, I mean that name alone," I joked. "It sounds pretty intimidating. I heard he owns a sport shop. How does he stay in business?" I hurried as I walked to the front of the store. The metal handle of the basket dug into my fingers.

"There aren't a lot of spots out here to get sports gear. The Laughing Gull Sport Shop sells it all. Fishing, scuba, hiking. And, to be fair, he does have good prices. I know Joe got a great deal on a tent and a couple of sleeping bags last summer when he took Colby and Christina out camping."

"Well, here's something you're going to think is weird. The air tank that Lenny was using had a gull sticker on it." I got into line and set the basket down on the conveyor belt with a sigh of relief.

Kari gasped. "Holy cow! That's the shop's trademark! Maybe Roy was finally ending the family feud. This might be the fastest murder mystery ever solved!"

I hoped she was right.

# CHAPTER 5

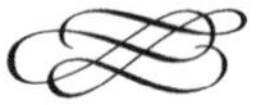

The rest of the evening was spent buttoned up in my cozy home. It really seemed like Lenny's murder was going to be solved quickly, a fact that appeared to be confirmed by Uncle Chris's text stating that the police had already released the property from the investigation.

I changed into my comfies—a pair of elastic-banded shorts and a t-shirt—and then started dinner. I stood on one leg, the other foot propped up against my knee, just like the famed flamingo mascot of our reality, as I stirred the spaghetti sauce.

I absolutely loved this kitchen. It was fun, and I could picture Mrs. Carmichael standing right here in this very spot while cooking her first meal as a married woman. There were still a lot of repairs to the place that needed to be done. Mrs. Carmichael had offered a discount on the rent if I'd paint and get rid of the wallpaper. It's true, it really had to go. There were roses and pink stripes everywhere. In fact, there was a strip dangling in the hallway that I had to resist yanking every time I walked by. The only reason I hadn't so far was that I wasn't one-hundred-percent sure I wanted to take on the challenge. But, one day, I was sure the temptation would be too great.

Just before I climbed into bed, I received an email from the realty website that another potential buyer had set up an appointment. I quickly confirmed the time with them and then started on my new favorite thing.

My great-great grandma Wiktoria's letters.

Dad had sent them to me when I'd first moved back to Pennsylvania in a care box. I'd been thrilled to receive them, a thrill that had shortly dissipated when I'd realized they were all written in Polish. But slowly, bit by bit, and with the help of Translate app, I was figuring out what they said.

Wiktoria had arrived from Poland during World War Two. She left her mother behind and these letters were Wiktoria's last communication with her.

They were precious to me. In fact, I'd found the perfect thing to keep them in at a second-hand store, a wooden box with a carved flower on top.

Gently, I spread out the one I'd been working on recently,

and then readied my paper and pen. I read it as best as I could and typed the words into the app. I pressed the translate button and wrote down the conversion. I had to guess a few times on what some of the letters were, but, after an hour, this is what I had.

*Dearest Momma,*

*How are you? I am well. You will be so happy to learn that I've found a good Catholic church. I walked to mass this morning. On the way, a man gave me a flower and told me I was very pretty. He made me smile, but don't worry, Momma. He's a good Catholic boy and works at the bakery. He said if I came by tomorrow he would have some day-old bread that I could have. I feel so fortunate.*

*I love my flat even though there are six of us in it. I have my bed under the stairs, but there is a window and a spot for a lamp and I'm happy. I also have a job. It's not much, but I mend clothes and wash them. You know the saying, never cry when it's raining outside.*

*I hope you are well. Much love,*

*Wiktoria.*

I sighed with a smile. She was such a courageous person. I loved piecing together her experiences as she tried to build a new life in an unfamiliar country. I rubbed my eyes and stretched, then rolled over and set the letter and pad on the table next to me. I was wiped out after today. My bed was calling to me and I couldn't resist. I scooted down on the pillow and pulled the sheets up to sleep.

---

THE NEXT MORNING felt like I was on a repeat cycle, with the deja vu feeling running strong as I headed back out to the Johnson's property for the new showing.

As I climbed out of the car, the wind grabbed my hair and spun it around. It didn't have the same cozy feel, whistling through the trees, like it had yesterday. I was scared to look at the lake, but I told myself I was being silly and forced myself. The water was as serene as a mirror, belying all the hidden horrors that had happened yesterday.

A white SUV turned into the driveway and parked behind me. I smiled firmly and straightened, getting my game face on.

Two young men got out.

"Hi, there. I'm Stella O'Neil," I said, striding forward to meet them with my hand out.

The first man had on a pair of slacks and some nice shoes. I eyed them with concern, knowing how muddy the property could be.

He reached for my hand. "Marty Davis. This is my younger brother, Jared."

The second man had short red hair and was dressed more casually in a t-shirt and jeans. He walked around the vehicle and shook my hand as well.

"Okay, well this is a great piece of property. Let me show you around," I said.

"You sure this is the place, bro?" Marty asked his brother.

My antennas went up. Oh, no. He'd heard about the murder.

"Yeah. This is it." Jared climbed up on a stump to look around.

"So, there was some excitement at that lake yesterday, huh?" Marty asked me. He grabbed his phone out and started to scan through it.

I nodded. "Unfortunately, there was a death. The police are still investigating, but the property has been cleared."

"Except for maybe a few ghosts," Jared said from the stump.

I laughed, hoping he was joking, and walked over to him.

"It's quite beautiful here, isn't it?" I said.

"Uh, yeah," said Jared. But he didn't seem very interested.

Instead his eyes swept across the shore like he was searching for something.

I was starting to feel a little off-kilter. Were all potential buyers this scattered when they viewed a home?

"Would you like to see inside the house?" I offered with a gesture toward the cabin. There was an empty Dr. Pepper can on the ground, probably left by somebody yesterday. I needed to remember to pick it up on my way out.

Then, I didn't have any more time to think about it. Jared jumped off the stump and strode off, yelling at his brother, "Hey, we need to get this done."

I followed behind feeling oddly like a tag-along rather than the leader of the group.

*Don't screw this up, Stella!* I warned myself. I adjusted my jacket and hurried after him.

"So, as you can see, the porch has been freshly painted," I said, with a gentle sweep of my hand.

"Mmm," said Marty, still staring at his phone.

"Have faith, this is it," said Jared, nudging Marty's arm.

I wrinkled my brow, then punched in the code in the lockbox hanging from the doorknob. The key dropped out and I unlocked the door. We walked inside.

A thick, musty scent wrapped around us like a wet scarf. Immediately, I mentally kicked myself for not having come in sooner. Duh! I should have aired it out, maybe even used a few air-fresheners. I swallowed hard, trying to think of how to explain this. Experience was sometimes a hard teacher.

"When has this place last been opened?" Jared asked, wrinkling his nose.

"Oh, I'm guessing maybe around a year ago. The owners actually live in New York."

"A year ago?" Marty repeated. He swept his fingers across the countertop and then wiped them on his pants, leaving behind a marked path in the dust on the surface.

"This place is a dump," Jared noted. He pulled a pack of gum from his pocket and unwrapped a piece. He shook his head as he glanced around the little living room. "Seriously, it'd be better just to doze it down." He balled up his gum wrapper and flicked it toward the kitchen.

The foil wrapper bounced along the floor and rolled to a stop in front of a cupboard door.

I smiled, stifling the urge to snap at him for littering. "Well, this place has lots of opportunity for whatever the new owners want to do." I pointed to a short hallway. "Back there are two small bedrooms, if you want to go check them out."

The men moseyed down the hall while I raced to scoop the wrapper up. As I reached down, something caught my attention.

The cupboard door was open a crack. I froze when I realized it was propped open by a pair of rubber flippers.

With my knuckle, I nudged the door open more. Were these here as a funny coincidence? Or were they used by the person who'd been with Lenny?

I glanced toward the bedrooms where the men could be heard laughing, and then pulled out my phone. Quickly, I zoomed in on the swim fins and snapped a picture. I forwarded it to my uncle with the words —**Look at what I found.**

A door slammed.

"So, Sarah!" Jared yelled.

I rolled my eyes but didn't bother to correct my name.

"Yes?" I said and bumped the cupboard shut with my knee.

"We want to get out of here and check the rest of the property, okay?"

"Absolutely! Just this way." I signaled to the front door. Both of the men stomped down the porch stairs.

"I'll be right out!" I yelled after them, and then rushed through the house to check that all the windows were locked.

I tried the back door, and discovered it was unlocked. Had it always been this way, or was this the door I heard shut? Everything else appeared secured.

"Hey, sweetie? You coming?" Marty asked.

*Yuck.* I plastered a smile on my face and closed the front door behind me. "I'm right here. Just need to make sure the place was locked up."

"Yeah, like someone would ever want to break into this shack." Jared snorted.

The smile froze on my face. I gritted my teeth, trying to ride the wave of self-control. Honestly, I didn't understand what their problem was. This place was cute. The house could even be added on to easily.

"Shall we continue to the lake?" I asked, stepping off the porch.

Without answering, Marty headed down with Jared close behind. I trailed at their heels, feeling my chances dwindling that this would actually lead to a sale.

My phone buzzed with a text from my uncle. **—Where'd you find it?**

I typed back.**—in the Johnson's cabin. You think it was from the murder?**

As luck would have it, just as I hit send, I stepped into a chuckhole. The phone flew in the air as my ankle twisted and I stumbled forward with a squeal.

The men never turned around. Mumbling silent curse words, I found my phone in the midst of some mucky leaves. Carefully, I tested my ankle. It seemed okay. I limped after them. I needed to ask if one of them had opened the back door, anyway.

The men were talking by the side of the lake as they stared out at the dark water. Quiet waves lapped at the shore.

"Secrets, secrets. Show me your secrets," said Jared. He spit his gum out into the water. The ripples circled across the surface.

"You sure about that?" Marty shielded his eyes from the sun and stared.

"That's what the riddle said."

*Wait, what? A riddle? What riddle?*

I hung back to give them space, hoping to learn more. But the men must have heard me because they both turned around at the same time.

"Hey, sweetie. This looks great," said Jared.

*I'm about to sweet him.* "Wonderful! Do you want me to write you up an offer?" I kept my tone crisp and professional.

"Eager, huh?" Marty nodded.

I smiled. "In full disclosure, I represent the seller. But I'd be happy to get this going for you."

"How long have you been in the business?" Marty asked. The two men started heading back up the hill.

I hesitated. Do I tell them? "I'm pretty new to the business."

"New, huh? How new?" asked Marty.

"Fairly," I hemmed.

"How many houses have you sold?" he pressed.

I wasn't sure legally what to do here, especially since I represented the seller. I swallowed and admitted. "This is my first."

Marty laughed and nudged Jared. "You hear that? You're her first."

"I've heard that before." He smirked and glanced at his watch. "Hey, are there any good bars in this town?"

Oh, boy. I hoped this wasn't a prelude to asking me out. "There's a great restaurant called White Rangers. It's out on Hobble road."

"I heard about that place. They have a new chef. Let me get the directions." Jared nodded. He took out his phone and typed.

"Yeah. That new chef is my buddy, Mike," Marty answered. And then to me, "Thank's for the tour. We'll get back to you." Without another look at the house, they climbed into their SUV, leaving me to wonder what that was all about.

As they backed out onto the road, I called Uncle Chris.

He answered on the first ring. "Yellow."

I cringed at his corniness. "Hey, Uncle Chris. What do I do about these swim fins? Should we call the police?"

"I already did. Somebody will be by later today to pick them up."

"So I can go?"

"Get out of there, slick."

# CHAPTER 6

It turns out, it was me that had to let the police into the Johnson's house to collect the swim fins. I'd already made it halfway home when Uncle Chris called to let me know. Groaning, I turned around.

By the time I arrived at the Johnson's house, Officer Taylor was waiting for me on the front porch, along with his partner. I had a feeling they'd been there for a while by the way their eyes narrowed as I walked up the stairs.

"Hi, I'm sorry to keep you waiting," I said, and punched in the code. The key dropped into my hand.

"Ma,am, I'm Officer Taylor. We met yesterday." The cop dipped his head slightly.

Was it only yesterday? It seemed like ages ago already.

The other officer said nothing, leaving me with an uncomfortable few seconds as I struggled to work the cold key in the door. *Unlock, unlock, unlock!*

Finally, the key worked, and the doorknob turned. There was an awkward moment when I started through at the same time as Officer Taylor, and we both jumbled in the doorway for a second before the cop stepped back.

"Sorry, it's just this way." I led them straight over to where I'd found the flippers.

They squatted down, and Officer Taylor opened the cupboard with a pen. The other cop shook open a bag. I have to admit, I was leaning over their shoulder in curiosity, searching for a clue about the owner's identity. They had a brand name, but no gull sticker this time. I supposed that would have been too easy.

Officer Taylor bagged the flippers, and then the two of them opened the rest of the cupboards and checked inside. One drawer held a pen that rolled forward as the drawer opened. But, since the house had been packed up a while ago, everything else was empty as expected.

When they finished, the officers walked through the rest of the rooms to check that the windows were secure in the same way I'd done earlier.

A few minutes later, they found me again.

"And you're the only one with a key?" Officer Taylor asked.

"Well, you saw how I got it. It's stored outside in the key box. Anyone who has the code can get in."

"Anyone? Who else knows the code?"

"Pretty much any realtor, I'm guessing," I answered with a small shrug. I remembered about the door. "The back door was unlocked earlier, but I was showing the place. The guys were down there and I thought I heard it close."

They gave each other a look and then Officer Taylor thanked me. They checked the back door again, and then headed outside to the front yard where they split up. Officer Taylor sauntered down to the lake while his partner circled the perimeter of the house.

Neither of them must have found anything of interest because, after a quick goodbye, they returned to their car. I sat on the steps and watched as they left.

Okay, that's done. I was a little unnerved at how Officer Taylor had asked me how someone could get in, and thought I'd better check the windows one more time.

Everything was shut up tighter than a turtle in its shell. I checked the kitchen window last. Through it, I could see the lake water becoming choppy. The wind must be picking up.

One by one, I closed the cupboard doors left open by the

cops, and then pushed the drawers shut. The last drawer jammed as I tried to shut it. I wiggled it a few times but it wouldn't slide in. I rolled my eyes and sighed. Great. It's broken.

I checked the drawer, but there was nothing in it that would cause the problem. Squatting, I opened the cupboard underneath and half-leaned in where I saw a paper stuck in the tracks. I reached and yanked it free, ripping it as I pulled.

I finally got it out and back on my feet. The first thing I noticed was a spicy scent. I brought the paper to my nose and sniffed. It was a man's cologne.

Hmm. I smoothed it flat on the counter where I noticed what appeared to me to be a man's handwritten mixture of print and cursive.

I squinted to decipher the chicken scratch.

*Sharp edge in watery grave. In west field for those that are brave. Through the woods and down the hole. Find it carefully, there's a toll.*

Goosebumps trickled up my arms. It sounded like some kind of treasure map. Was this the riddle Marty and Jared were referring to? Or another weird coincidence?

Well, something was going on here. As soon as I moved my hand, the paper immediately wanted to curl back into a roll, stopped only by a crimp from being stuck in the cupboard. That was another thing; why was the paper rolling? I'd never seen anything like it. The scent coming from it was powerful, and actually yummy. Definitely like a guy I wouldn't mind getting to know better.

I dropped the paper tube into my purse, feeling a little foolish, like I was gathering someone's garbage and saving it. But a man did get murdered here. I wanted to be careful with any clues.

The house shook under a gust of wind. I glanced out the window to see a dark line on the horizon blowing in. The sudden graying light made me realize I really didn't want to be out here alone. I tucked my purse over my shoulder and ran out of the house.

After locking the front door, I double-checked to make sure the key was secure in the realty box. The wind spun my hair around my face, blinding me. Tree branches creaked and leaves tumbled. I scooped my hair back with one hand and rushed for the car.

The car door gave me a little trouble trying to unlock it. Once opened, I jumped inside and slammed the door. Good grief! The temperature sure had dropped. I started the car and flipped on the heat.

I rubbed my hands together in front of the vents, waiting for the car to warm up. Soon the heat was blasting and I flipped the vent to blow on me. I wasn't sure where my chill came from, the cold wind, or just being alone at the same location where I'd found a dead body.

The body. I stared out at the lake again. Over the years, two people had died in that dark water, linked together by bloodlines. The original owner, and now his grandson. The waves lapped at the shore harder as if trying to escape its border.

I shivered and stepped on the gas to pull out of the driveway. The flamingo greeted me with a cocky turn of his head. I noticed the mailbox flag broken and hanging on the metal box, and remembered the mailman from the other day. Slowly, I rolled up to and opened the door of the box, frowning when I discovered it was just junk mail. I left it and drove out on to the road.

So, this riddle thing. It couldn't have been a coincidence to find it after hearing Marty and Jared talking. I couldn't even guess how the paper got into the house, but I knew I needed to learn more about this riddle. Was it a common one, some well-known children's poem that I'd somehow missed growing up? Maybe it was some local lore that only the Brookfield people knew.

Twenty minutes later, I turned onto my rather isolated dirt road. I passed the white farmhouse of my nearest neighbor tucked way off the road. Bales of hay dotted the yard all around the neighbor's house. The storm's gloomy light spread a silvery cast over the dry straw. It was funny how, in the summer, I had barely been able to see their house through the waving green. Only the peaked roof had shown above the crops.

The car shook. *Wow!* That wind was strong! I blew out a sigh of relief when I turned down my driveway. The trees in the yard swayed in the windy battle. I watched with my stomach knotting. *Dear God, don't let any hit the house!*

I got out and raced to the covered porch. Just as I reached the front door, rain fell with fat splats that hissed in the dry dirt. Laughing at beating the storm, I unlocked the door, and made a beeline straight for the kitchen to make some tea and find a flashlight. I definitely wanted to be prepared if the power went out.

As if releasing pent-up energy, the rain dumped from the sky. It was oddly comforting to hear it pound the roof. I carried a mug of tea to a beat-up couch by the window and squirreled myself in with my legs tucked up.

It was strangely beautiful outside. It had been a while since the last storm, and I almost could feel the earth greedily sucking in the water. There's a scent that accompanies a late downpour, dark and sensuous, a mixture of green life and growth, and rich earth.

I breathed in and remembered how my feet splashed through puddles, splatters of mud dotting my bare legs. I'd raced mid-distance in high school—a one mile run—and went on to do one year of track in college.

The unwelcome memory of my last race rolled over me and my chin dropped to my knees. It was the moment my ego received its first real beating.

I never realized before that I was a case of being a big fish in a small pond. In college, the sprinters came from all around the country on scholarships. I suddenly went from winning every race to coming in fifth. Eighth. Ninth.

A huge part of my identity died that day I came in ninth place. I knew then that I was nobody special. I wasn't this great track star that I'd once taken pride in.

I quit the team (much to their relief, I think) and then clung with everything I had to keep my identity as a great scholar. I fought for it. I couldn't lose that, no matter what. And so, to the detriment to any social life or friends, I lived for those grades.

To this day, I never told a soul how much it scared me to realize that I was just average athlete. That moment, I'd felt like a kite caught in a strong wind who'd been snapped from their string.

I sipped my coffee and watched the leaves fly through the air like my imagined kite. Tumbling, turning, and no amount of putting your mind to it was going to change that. I guess, in some ways, I was still waiting to see where I was going to land.

Finally, I grabbed my phone. It was time to search out the riddle. I might not exactly know the answer to the big question of 'why I was here', but I was here now. This was what was on my plate, and I was going to do my best with it.

I typed in the riddle and stretched my neck, as if I could shrug off the melancholy reminiscing just as easily. Okay. Moving forward. I just wanted to see if the riddle was common knowledge or not.

The spinny thing did its thing and then a row of options popped up.

What I read made my mouth drop.

# CHAPTER 7

Lightning forked across the sky and thunder battered the house, making the windows shake. I scooted away from the window and read the words on the internet again. I'd found my poem all right, and it was listed on a page called Unsolved Riddles.

My phone rang, erasing the search. I yelped in dismay. There was no phone number, instead it displayed *unknown*.

Irritated, I answered it. "Hello?"

The man on the other end sounded just as impatient as I felt. "Hey, I saw this house by a lake online, and this is the listing phone number."

Listing number? I didn't put my phone number online. What was he talking about?

He rapidly fired out, "I was wondering if it would be okay to come see it. Like now, maybe?"

The power flickered as if to protest his words. He had to be kidding. The weather was terrible. Did someone really expect me to go tromp out in this storm?

Still, it wouldn't do to tell a possible sale that they were crazy. I answered in my most diplomatic tone, "It's getting kind of late today. Let's set up an appointment for tomorrow."

"Okay, I guess so." He drawled out reluctantly. "Is eight in the morning too early?"

Eight o'clock? That was the crack of dawn! I rubbed my neck and mustered up some enthusiasm, "Absolutely. Do you have the address?"

"Yep. I sure do."

"Okay, we'll meet there, then." After hearing his assent, I hung up.

That was strange. He sounded young, too.

The phone rang again, oscillating like a baby rattlesnake in my hand. Lovely. Another unknown number. Since when had I become Miss Popular?

"Hello. This is Stella O'Neil."

"Hi! I'd like to set up a time to check out a piece of property on your site," a man answered back.

A chill ran down my back. *No way.* I'd heard of hot properties, but how was this one so popular? Because of the murder?

"Okay," I said hesitantly.

"You available now?" He sounded young as well. I swear, I could hear gum smacking in his mouth.

"No, I'm sorry. The first available appointment I have is nine tomorrow morning. Will that work for you?"

He took a deep breath. "I guess so. Listen, do you have a lot of other people interested?"

"The property has garnered some interest." Not the best way to answer, maybe, but the call-waiting on my phone was cutting in and distracting me.

"I'd really, really like to be the first one out there. If you could just make an exception."

"Nine tomorrow," I said firmly.

By the time I got off the phone the third call had gone to voice mail.

As I listened to it—another young-sounding man—the phone

rang a fourth time. I stared at it and pressed ignore. Then I called my uncle.

“Hello?” He sounded stressed.

“Uncle Chris? I’ve just had four phone calls to see the Johnson’s property in the last five minutes. Holy Cow, I’m getting another one right now. How are they getting my number? What’s going on?”

“They’re calling the line that we have forwarding to your phone. I’m sorry, I meant to tell you that, earlier. I have no idea what’s happening. My email is jammed full of requests, with more adding like they’re rabbits in the springtime.”

“What the heck? Is it because of the murder?”

“Honestly, I’ve never seen anything like it. I’m calling the police and see if they can have someone run out there and make sure there isn’t some weird gathering taking place. This is crazy!”

There was nothing more to say, and it was infuriating anyway with the calls I was still getting. We said goodbye, and I hung up.

I switched on my Do Not Disturb setting, and blew out my cheeks. This was insanity. Something new had to have transpired.

Rubbing my forehead, I scrolled back to the online article.

Inane music started playing as a long list opened up. The site boasted that these were the top one hundred riddles of all time. The list seemed pretty conclusive, with everything from who was being secretly referred to in song lyrics, to scavenger hunts that no one had been able to solve.

My poem was listed at number eighty-seven.

There was no explanation underneath it, just the poem. As I read it again, I noticed the words were slightly different than the ones in my note.

*Sharpest edge in a watery grave. Over the west field for those that are brave. Through the woods and down the hole. Take it carefully and beware of the toll.*

The difference between the two reminded me of the shorthand I'd used to take notes in college, jotting down the gist of what I'd heard. Maybe the person who had written this had done the same thing.

Questions filled my thoughts, one after the other. First of all, what did this have to do with the Johnson's property? Was there really some sort of treasure in the flooded house? And how in the world could the public have connected Johnson Lake to this very vague poem? And why this week of all weeks? Old Man Lenny must have connected it too. Who had he told? Was it that person who had followed him into the water?

It seemed pretty important to figure out if this riddle was associated or not.

The phone rang again, surprising me. Then, I realized it was my dad. I had rigged my phone that he could always get through, even if the Do Not Disturb setting was on.

There was a second where I considered not answering it. Conversation wasn't always easy with him, and I wasn't so sure I wanted to tackle it now. We'd been getting along better, it was true, but nothing changed the fact that he wasn't happy that I'd moved from Seattle and was back in Pennsylvania, and he wasn't shy about making his feelings known. Not to mention, he always honed in on my emotions if I was upset or worried, like a bee to a buttercup. He definitely wouldn't be happy about me discovering a murdered man.

Still, it was my dad. So, of course, I answered it, using my breeziest voice. "Hi, Dad."

There was a pause, like he'd been preparing to leave a message, and me actually answering caught him off guard. "Stella." After clearing his throat, he said more firmly, "How are you?"

"I'm good, Dad. What are you doing? How are you?"

Lighting flashed in the window and thunder rumbled. I flinched and quickly amended it with, "Actually, I'm in the middle of an electrical storm. Lighting just tried to get in through the window, I swear."

"Oh. I see. Well, you can call me back. I just—."

"No, Dad. Seriously, its good to hear from you."

"Same here. Actually, I was just calling to tell you that I miss you."

"Aww, I miss you too, Dad. You want to come out soon?" I eyed the ripped wallpaper and chewed my nail, waiting nervously for his response.

"It'd be hard for me to go back there, hun. So many memories." He didn't verbalize it but I knew he meant my mom and his dad. He still hadn't talked to Oscar in all these years since we moved.

My dad assumed that I'd try to contact my grandfather, but I never actually confirmed it with him. I decided to poke around a bit to see if now was the time to let him know. "You know, I think it would be good for you to come out. Kind of confront the past so it didn't have power over you anymore."

I held my breath, not sure if I'd gone too far.

He groaned. "Stella..."

"I'm sorry, Dad. I know it's hard for you."

"No, it's just....Maybe you're right."

My jaw dropped. Let me tell you, I couldn't have been more shocked if a monkey ran through the room. In all the years I'd known my dad, I'd never heard him admit that someone else was right. Not me nor anyone else.

"Dad, What's going on? Are you feeling okay?" Adrenaline flushed through me. That was it. Something had to be wrong with him. I needed to get back there to Washington right away. Did he just get some bad news from the doctor?

"Honey. I feel fine. It's just that I'm realizing how parenthood is a cruel trick. You spend all these years trying to protect your kid. You do everything you can to be responsible and keep them safe. And then, one day, you have to let go. There's nothing in the parenting manual that prepares you for that."

"Dad, you did a great job." I said, and I meant it. After a second, I added, "Oscar thinks so, too."

There. The band-aid was ripped off. I twisted a piece of my hair nervously, wondering what he would say next.

I didn't have to wait for long.

"Well, how would he know that?" His voice had its usual acerbic bite when talking about Oscar, but it also sounded like he really was curious. Let's see. How to word this... Well, Dad, you know how you've tried to keep the last twenty years private from Oscar? Well, I've been sharing those memories of growing up with him.

Nope, not going to do it. I took the easy way out.

"We've talked a few times. He mentioned once that he could tell you did a good job."

"Did he now?" Dad harrumphed. "Well, he always did like to dig out the truth. So, you're doing okay, then?"

I thought about the dead body, the million phone calls I'd just received, and what might be buried treasure sitting at my first house up for sale. His head would figuratively explode if he knew. Instead, I said, "Totally! Things are going great right now."

"All right. You call me soon. Got that?"

"Soon. I promise."

Little did I know that'd be a promise I'd have to break.

# CHAPTER 8

After my phone call with my dad, I grabbed my new notebook—one with a fabulous embossed cover—and opened it to the first fresh page. *Okay, Mr. Riddle. Tell me your secrets.*

I found my way back to the Unsolved Riddles list and scrolled down to number eighty-seven. I copied and pasted it into a separate search bar and hit enter. I wanted to see if the correct wording would yield anything new.

The rainbow wheel spun as the page tried to load. Now I was getting irritated with the weather. It was interfering with the wi-fi. The rain beat against the window in an epitome of the term *lashing*, with zero signs of ending soon.

I tapped my pen against the paper and then glanced at the

search bar. The only link that finally showed up led back to the site I'd just left. No help at all.

Okay, what else could I try? Well, if the lake's the answer, I might as well dig into its history.

The Johnson Lake name brought up several links, the first being the story of how it got made. Yeah, yeah, yeah. Blah, blah, blah. Nothing new here.

But the next one was surprising. It was a link to a gamer's site.

Why in the world would this lake be mentioned on a gamer's site?

I clicked on the name, Trek's World, which led to a giant forum. As someone whose idea of a big game was Sudoku, I was immediately overwhelmed. I hadn't heard of any of these. Even worse, each game had its own mini forum filled with posts.

At the top of the page was a search function. Keeping my fingers figuratively crossed, I typed in the lake's name. Honestly, if this didn't work, I wasn't sure what else to try. There would be no way I could sift through this massive sea of posts.

The screen went blank as it brought up the searches.

*Come on. Come on.*

A link popped up to a thread named "Relic found at a garage sale!"

Even more interestingly, the date was marked three days ago. Excitement zinged through me as I hurriedly clicked it and scrolled through the comments.

—Anyone hear the news of what was discovered at some random garage sale this weekend? You know the riddle, *Sharpest edge in a watery grave. Over the west field for those that are brave. Through the woods and down the hole. Take it carefully and beware of the toll.* Well, I know the guy who found a book called "Through the Woods," and that poem was in it! Signed by the author, Ava Summers. It said, "Once my home was safe. Now the water laps the grave."

Another person responded—You're behind, son. I looked up the author and it said her father's home was flooded years ago. It's Johnson's Lake. I'm heading there to check it."

I practically vibrated from excitement. This was it! All the other posts after that one chimed in with congratulations and their own interpretation of the riddle.

I knew it. People were coming to see if this property was the answer to the riddle. If people believed there really was a treasure down in the lake, then they'd be making offers on the property. Whoever owned it would own the treasure.

But after yesterday, was the treasure even down there anymore?

I scrolled back up to find the original poster's name. GettingStamped.

What a weird screen name. I needed to talk to him. I really did. Now, how could I find who this person really was?

I didn't see any way to message him on the site. But, there was a link that said, register now, so I made an account. Everything was going well until I had to come up with my own screen name. My fingers froze over the keyboard. What the heck should I put?

I went back to the games I'd played as a kid and typed in CarmenS, for Carmen Sandiego. Then I hit enter.

An option to message him popped up. I bit my lip and gave a stupid grin as I typed. "Hey I saw your post and I was wondering if you'd been able to check if there was a real connection to Johnson Lake or not. I have a link to it. Message me as soon as you can. People are crawling all over the place."

I hit *send* and held my breath. I don't know why I was so anxious. He might not get back to me for days. To check that theory out, I clicked his profile to see when he'd last logged in. Three days ago. I groaned. He might never answer me.

It brought me back to the fact that Old Man Lenny was no

spring chicken. He didn't seem to be the type that would be interested in a gamer's site. It didn't make sense why he went to the lake after this post was made.

I needed to get more information about Lenny. Was he married? Did he have kids? Quickly, I jotted down the questions so that I'd remember to get the answers in the morning. Then I rinsed out my mug and got my laundry going. I figured I had some things to get in order before it was time for bed. Maybe I'd even bake some cookies. I could use the sugar fortification.

After all, tomorrow was going to be an important day.

# CHAPTER 9

It wasn't an easy night sleep, what with the storm outside and the one brewing in my head. I finally gave up at six am, and stumbled into the kitchen blinking bleary eyes. I swallowed a couple of aspirin and then scuffed over to my couch, gripping my mug of coffee like it was the holy grail. The coffee was hot, nearly burning my mouth. But I savored it, blowing and taking small sips as I watched the rain splash in the mud puddles.

I thought about my grandfather, sitting all alone in his own house. Maybe even watching the rain like I was. Was he lonely? He'd seen a lot. I didn't know what he thought of his sons, my dad and Uncle Chris. I wasn't sure where he was with wanting to reconcile.

The last time I'd talked with Uncle Chris, he'd sounded like he thought there was no hope. That the distance between everyone had been too much for far too long.

I couldn't hear it. I wouldn't accept it. I needed this, needed everyone to get back together. And I had a seed of faith that it was going to happen.

Despite my weird upbringing, I realized that maybe I was an old soul who was super nostalgic. I guess I was always that way. When I was a kid, Dad would take me to see Santa at Cabela's. I saw the same Santa every year until I was eleven when I refused to take any more Santa pictures. I was too old, I'd insisted. But I also made Dad continue to take me the first weekend of every December. Ostensibly, I was looking for Dad's Christmas present, but really, I wanted to walk by the Grandpa-like man I'd seen since I was six years old. It made my holiday to watch him say, "Merry Christmas! Ho! Ho! Ho!"

I think he remembered me. When I'd walk by, he'd lift a gloved-hand and wave with the time-hewn jolly twinkle of his eye. Then he'd give me a wink and a thumbs up.

I always waved back and ducked my head with a smile.

I thought of the phone call with my dad last night, and took another sip. The rich coffee scent filled me with ease. It had been good to hear his voice. I really did want him to come up and see my place.

My eye caught sight of the peeling wallpaper. Just as soon as I had *that* fixed.

Sighing, I got up and refilled my cup, then hung up a load of laundry up on a wooden drying rack that I'd forgotten in the washer.

Finished, I sank before the computer with a yogurt and opened my email.

My eyes popped open. There was a long string of emails from Uncle Chris. I clicked the most recent.

He wrote, "Why aren't you answering your phone?"

I smacked my forehead as I remembered that I'd turned on the Do Not Disturb setting last night. Quickly, I flipped it off. Staring at the phone, I considered calling him. Was it too early? Sometimes, he liked to stay out with his old racing buddies. I groaned and sent him a text instead. **—Sorry! What's going on?**

I watched the phone for a second but there was no answer. Yeah, he must still be in bed.

There was also a message from Kari, asking me to stop the realty on my way to Johnson Lake.

Well, no more horsing around. I had that eight o'clock appointment and one right after that. After reading the forum, I didn't have a lot of hope any of these were legit buyers, but it was still going to be a busy day.

When I arrived at Flamingo Realty, her silver minivan was already parked outside. She was seated behind her desk and looked up as I came in.

"Miss Popularity," she said with a smile. She grabbed the papers in front of her and rifled them into a stack. "Just the person I wanted to see."

"You heard about that, huh?" I said. "What are you doing?"

Kari handed me a piece of paper. "I was about to text this to you. This is what came through on the Flamingo website last night."

I glanced at the paper. There was a list of names and numbers that had booked showings. I made a face as I read it. I should have packed a lunch.

"Uncle Chris said he asked the police to swing by last night and make sure no one was out there partying or something. Any news about that?" I asked.

"I didn't hear anything, so I assume it's fine."

"So, I have a couple of questions. What's the deal with this guy, Lenny? Did he have a family?"

"No, he never married. I have no idea why. He was a nice

guy," Kari said. "He used to be in the barbershop quartet. I remember them singing at the nursing home last Christmas season when I was visiting my grandma. They did such a cute job." She smiled at the memory. "Grandma flirted with him a bit. He was a great sport and let her kiss his cheek."

"Aw, that's cute. So, where did he live exactly?"

"He lived on the ranch of that restaurant I was telling you about. Had a room there. I don't know much more about him, other than he seemed to enjoy his job."

"So, why would Roy Merlock not like him?"

"A hundred years ago, it was over water rights. Their families have been feuding ever since, even after the Johnson's sold the property. Who knows what fuels these family feuds." She shrugged.

"You want to know what's creepy? Whoever killed Lenny was in the water with him. They must have been friends."

Kari tucked her short blonde hair behind her ear. "Or the person knew that Lenny was going to be there and showed up when he was already in the water."

Well, that was a new theory I hadn't considered. "I heard the Johnson's house flooded before they could get everything out. Do you think there's some kind of treasure down in the house still?"

Kari laughed. "I hardly think so. Besides, over a hundred years have passed since that happened. Who knows how many people have been in that water, snooping around that old house. If there were anything there, it would have been found ages ago."

I nodded. Not to mention, I could hardly imagine what someone could have all those years ago that gamers would want. My gaze landed on the clock on the wall, igniting a flare of panic. I needed to haul butt over there or I would miss the showing.

I ran for the door, shouting, "Holy cow, I'm late! I'll talk to you later."

"Hang on a second, Stella," Kari called. I cringed and turned around, not having time for small talk.

"There's another thing really weird about all this sudden interest in the house."

"What?" I asked.

"None of these people who've made appointments have an agent representing them. They're just coming straight to you."

"Is that strange?" I asked. I wouldn't know since this was my first sale.

"Yeah, it really is." Her brows rumpled. I didn't know what to say in response, so I waved goodbye and ran to my car.

I might be running late, but I had to get something to eat, so I whipped through the drive through. Ten minutes later, while munching on an egg wrap, I thought about what Kari said. Up until now I'd been pleased there was no other real estate agent involved. It was a no brainer—more commission for me.

But now I felt like it was more proof that these people weren't interested in buying the property after all. They were just using me to snoop around. I was glad Uncle Chris had called the police to have them keep an eye on the place, and I was starting to wonder what I was going to find when I got there.

## CHAPTER 10

My gut instincts were right on the money. It was not a pretty sight when I pulled into the driveway and jockied my car into a space to park. Three cars were already there, with a fourth following behind me. I flushed with outrage when I saw a crowd of people down by the lake. There were people in the water, people running up the shore. There was even someone up in a tree.

There was no time for a text. I called Uncle Chris.

As I got out of the car, phone to my ear, a woman in a business suit stalked toward to me. Her expensive high heels stabbed into the ground, looking about as out of place as a fine china cup in a pig pen. As if to prove my point, her heel speared a mud clot like a shish-kabob. Her front deepened when she had to stop to shake it off.

"You never got back to me," she shrilly accused, her brows raising even more. "What kind of professionalism is that?"

I held up a finger to signal to her to wait just one minute. Uncle Chris had answered.

"Uncle Chris? Send some help immediately."

He exhaled heavily. "Stella?" he asked, his voice muffled. I realized then that I'd woken him up.

"It's kind of a nonemergency emergency. This place is flooded with people and....oh my gosh, here comes another... I'm calling the police for trespassing."

The woman continued to harp at me. I walked around the car with her hot on my heels.

"Where are you?" he asked.

"At the Johnson's house! It's a zoo here!" I yelled, wanting to reach through the phone and yank him over here to see this mess.

"Oh. Right." There was a lot of rustling and he grunted. "Okay, I'm on my way. I'll give Dave a call."

"Wait, what? Who's Dave?"

"He's that friend of mine down at the station. He'll get someone out pretty quick. Don't worry." I heard a thump, then he continued. "I'll be there in fifteen minutes."

"All right. Bye." I didn't have time to talk anymore. The woman had reached me, never once pausing in her ranting, and was actually jabbing her finger in my direction. I didn't have the fortitude to focus on what she was saying, because sounds of splashing made me turn back to the lake. More men waded in, some with snorkel masks.

I clutched the phone like it was my life line, my mouth hanging open.

There was a tap on my shoulder. I turned to see the woman mere inches from my face with her finger. I stepped back, one second away from swatting it like a fly.

"I expected a phone call back. I've never had someone treat me this way before!" the woman harped.

I just couldn't deal with her. I held my finger up again and dialed Kari.

"Stella, you okay?" She must have heard the yells in the background because her voice was immediately on guard.

"Nope. Not in the slightest. You think you could head this way?"

"Yeah. Of course. What's going on?"

"Let's just say my cup overfloweth with buyers."

"Oh, boy. That bad huh?"

"Ms. O'Neil," screech the woman.

Kari was silent for a second and then stated, "I'm on my way."

Okay. I'd called in the troops, and now all I could do was wait. I took a deep breath and turned toward the woman. Her eyes glared, supercharged with emotion. I'm sure ruining her shoes didn't help.

"And what is this circus?" she asked, waving her hands. Just as she said this, yet another car pulled into the driveway.

"Who are you, again?" I asked as she finally took a breath.

Her mouth dropped, appearing actually shocked that I'd asked that. "I'm Angela Cranton, with Cranton Realty. We have an appointment?"

At that moment, five more people climbed out of the car. One with yet another metal detector.

I groaned as I saw them. "Everything is quite odd right now, I'll give you that," I said to her and marched over to the car. "Hey, guys!" I waved my hands to get their attention. "Sorry. No one's allowed on the property without being represented by a real estate agent."

"They don't have an agent?" The harpy woman had followed me. She raised her hand and gave them the biggest smile. "Hi there, I'll be happy to represent you!"

I glared at her. "Do they look interested in buying a house to you?" And then back to the men, "Get back in your car. Go find an agent."

They ignored me, with only one giving me a very dismissive glance, as they walked to the lake. I stamped my foot, infuriated. "The police are on their way." I yelled after them. "If you don't leave you will be arrested for trespassing."

"What about them?" The guy who'd glanced at me asked as he pointed to the group by the lake.

"I'm getting to them. Now you guys get out of here before the cops come."

"I've never seen a real estate agent drive buyers off the property before," the woman next to me grumped. I glared at her as she kicked yet another mud clot off her shoe.

"Do you have a real client?" I asked.

"What? Of course, I do." She lifted her chin indignantly.

"Where are they, then?"

"I left them on the front porch." She turned to look. "Oh. They were right there. I'm not sure...." She spun around, trying to track them down.

I resisted the urge to roll my eyes. "You go find your clients while I get those people out of the water."

"What is going on here?" she asked.

I sighed. "I'm not entirely sure." Then I grimly marched down to the lake, muttering to myself. "But I'm going to find out."

As I walked to the shore, I saw someone kick toward the center of the lake. His buddy was thigh deep in the water and adjusting his mask when I reached the shoreline.

"Hey! Over here!" I yelled.

The man looked up.

"Come out of there and talk to me." I waved my arms like I was marking the runway for a jumbo jet.

He glanced at his friend, just a blob and a snorkel from this distance, and then back at me.

"That's right. Come here right now. The cops are on their way."

As if to punctuate my sentence, a bull horn blasted behind me. I nearly peed myself and jumped to turn.

Speak of the devil. A cop keyed up his loudspeaker. "This is the police. Get out of the water."

The man yanked his snorkel free and cupped his hands to yell at his friend. "Jerry! Jerry! Get out of the water!"

Well, Jerry, if that really was his name, didn't hear his friend and continued deeper.

The cop shut his car door and walked toward us. The guy in front of me cussed under his breath and began wading toward the shore. I glanced around for the other group of people but they had scattered at the sight of the cop like mice when the light flips on. I caught just a glimpse of someone running through the brush.

Just then, the real estate agent popped up. She stood on the porch and yelled, "Yoo-hoo! I found them! We're ready when you are!"

# CHAPTER 11

It was Officer Taylor who showed up again, and I think he was getting sick of seeing me so often. The feeling wasn't mutual as I practically pranced over to his side. I nearly hugged him, I was so grateful he was there. Between the blast of his siren a few times, and his uniform, he had most of the trespassers gathered together—the only one missing was Jerry who still floated out in the lake. I stood on the fringes of the group, listening.

"What are you guys doing here?" the cop asked. He was a picture of authority, his feet wide apart, his shoulders squared to match his stance.

Now that was the million dollar question. I held my breath, wondering if my hunch was right.

I wasn't sure I was going to get my answer. The trespassers rubbed the backs of their neck and stared at one another, shifting their feet.

Officer Taylor raised an eyebrow. "I can easily call in the wagon and have you all brought to the station. I don't mind asking my questions down there. I will remind you, trespassing is a crime. Your choice, boys."

The young men bounced glances off of each other. Finally, one of them spoke up. "We just want to find the sword."

A sword? "What are you talking about?" I asked.

Officer Taylor's eyes flicked toward me in annoyance but I ignored him. I was so close! Just give me the confirmation I need!

No one responded, so I prompted, "Are you here because of the riddle?" *Come on, come on, come on!*

One kid, with long shaggy hair rolled his eyes. "Yeah. The riddle. Whatever. It led us here. You know the sword. It's in all the ancient role-playing games. It's cool."

I actually giggled, so satisfied to finally know the truth. Then, realizing how I'd interrupted, I ducked my head in apology toward Officer Taylor.

Officer Taylor went over rules of private property and gave a basic lecture. To be honest, I was tuning him out. If there was a sword on the property, did Lenny know about it, being that it was in his family? And if so, why did he wait to go after it now, after all these years?

"Stella!" Uncle Chris yelled. He waved at me.

Seeing him was almost as good as seeing my dad. I can't explain the relief and happiness that flooded through me as I ran over to him. As I got closer, I saw that Kari had arrived also. She was on the porch, talking with Angela Cranton. Joining the two of them was another couple.

"You okay?" Uncle Chris asked when I reached him. He grabbed me into a hug as if to make sure I wasn't missing a limb or hurt in some way.

"I'm so glad you're here! You can't even believe how crazy it's been. That cop over there is interviewing the ones still dumb enough to stay and get caught." I pointed out to the lake. "And out there is some wahoo still happily snorkeling with no idea of what's going on."

Uncle Chris scowled as he stared out at the lake. He plucked a cigar from his pocket and bit off the end. He spat and said, "I guess I need to see what we're going to do about Aquaman. Does anyone have any idea what's going on?"

"So, last night I stumbled onto a gamer's site. It was talking about this lake as the answer to an old pun. They think an ancient sword is down in the water. Ask Officer Taylor. He was twisting the screws a bit to find out more."

"Okay." His thick eyebrows flicked toward the house. "You go take care of that showing. They might be legit. And they must really want this place to stick around despite the dog-and-pony show. Let's get this house sold as fast as we can and out of our hair."

He snapped his lighter and puffed a few times. When his cigar was going, he squelched through the mud toward the cop while I headed to the house.

Kari's voice carried over as I approached the porch. It was carefree and exuded confidence, "Ahh, here she is. See, I told you that she had everything under control. Now that's a good real estate agent." She grinned, all her teeth showing. I raised my eyebrows at the maniacal smile, pretty sure I could conclude how the conversation had gone while I was busy.

I walked up the stairs and was quickly introduced to a Mr. and Mrs. Harris. They were a nice couple from St. Petersburg.

"And interestingly enough Stella, Mrs. Cranton and I went to school together," Kari said, beaming that same phony beauty-pageant smile.

The two real estate agents giggled at each other and touched each other's elbows in good humor. Fake, cold, and brittle good humor.

"So," I addressed to the Harrises. "It has been a little nuts around here but everything is settling down now. Have you had a chance to check out the house yet?"

"Yes. Mrs. Cranton has taken us through." Mr. Harris smiled at his agent. I wasn't sure if he was sucking up so he'd get a deal on the house, but I could tell him he could skip that part. I was more than ready to encourage our seller to negotiate and be done with this sale.

"Terrific. Did you have any questions?" It was something I hated to ask. How could they not be dubious, especially with all these strangers combing the land? Not to mention Free-Willy out there bobbing in the waves.

The two of them shook their heads, which made me so grateful I'd even be willing to knock another quarter point off my commission.

"Don't worry. I've told them everything they'd need to know. I'm actually taking them to another house." Mrs. Cranton sniffed. I had no idea people did that outside of Regency films. "Some place represented by a professional," she added, give me the eye up and down.

"Well, hey, now!" Kari shook her head. "Stella is every bit of a professional. This has been a rather unusual situation."

"Unusual!" Mrs. Cranton laughed. "I should say so. The way she's run this showing has been more of a college rave than something my company represents. Of course if you trained her, maybe that's to be expected."

Kari and I both froze.

"Ta-Ta, Kari. Call me when you're ready to really break into the business." Mrs. Cranton waggled her fingers. The Harrises followed behind her, looking rather embarrassed and confused.

I could almost feel the heat from Kari's fuming, like someone had dumped gasoline on a fire. Mrs. Cranton tried to back out her car, only to lose traction. Her tires spun in the mud, and Kari's expression lightened. Mrs. Cranton shifted forward and attempted to back out again, this time with no trouble.

We watched the car disappear down the road.

"I hate her, hate everything about her. Hate her hair and her clothes and her stupid smile," Kari spat out.

"So, tell me how you really feel," I joked, still feeling shocked at how horrible that woman was.

Kari gave me an angry side-eye. "She's always been like that."

"Always?"

"Even in school. Especially in school. She was the kid who

picked on the other kids, who had the rich parents and the latest and greatest everything."

The vitriol flamed through Kari's voice and was a poignant reminder at how memories from even that far back could still sting so strongly.

"At least she didn't call you an incompetent agent who hosts college Frat parties," I said, dryly.

Kari started to laugh. "She's a piece of work, I'll tell you. Maybe you should be glad you lost that sale."

"Yeah? Well, did you see her face when I walked up? Like she was smelling an overflowing outhouse. Does she always look like that?"

Kari raised an eyebrow. "You know that warning all moms use, about your face getting stuck that way? I'm pretty sure that's happened to her. Sour puss extraordinaire."

We both laughed then, though I couldn't tell if it was at the realty agent or the sheer absurdity of the day.

Officer Taylor approached us, followed by a group of young men, including a new man wearing a wet suit. Uncle Chris slowly meandered behind, puffing out a cloud of smoke.

"Apparently, they got Flipper out of the water," I whispered to Kari.

She laughed harder and tried to hide it behind her hand.

The young men split off and headed to their cars. One by one, they drove away. I breathed a huge sigh of relief when the last one left.

“All right, you guys. So you have a plan then?” Officer Taylor asked.

Uncle Chris took out the cigar, the end soggy and chewed. “Yeah. I talked to the owners on the way here. I’m calling in a scuba diving expert and a security team. We’ll have this all sorted out within the next day or two.”

The cop nodded. “Get it squared away. We’ll keep patrolling it, but we don’t have the resources to do this long term.”

“Thank you for your help, sir.” Uncle Chris shook his hand.

The officer left, and then we were alone. The wind howled, the trees creaked, and the lake rippled.

“Well, that was fun,” Uncle Chris said. “Who needs coffee?”

# CHAPTER 12

We did get that coffee together, which turned into a lovely chat at a cafe table outside Darcy's Doughnuts. Uncle Chris filled me in with some more news about his plans to eventually run for city mayor.

"If you really want to run, you're going to have to endear Flamingo Realty to the community," I said, before taking a sip of my chai tea.

"Endear? What's more endearing than a flamingo?"

"Well, they feel like we're just here for a money grab. Maybe you could do something to show you want to give back to the town."

His brow rumpled as he thought about it, and he shoved a big bite of glazed doughnut into his mouth.

"Maybe like a picnic, you know with a bouncy house," Kari suggested.

"A bouncy house?" Uncle Chris shot her a surprised look. "Isn't that something you'd find in Vegas?"

I snorted, nearly shooting tea out my nose. Kari rolled her eyes.

"What?" He turned to me.

"I don't even want to know the places you go to that you'd think that's an adult activity," I said, shaking my head.

"Honestly, a bouncy house. It's inflatable. Kids go in and jump...." Kari spoke in dragged out words like she was explaining to a toddler.

"Oh, yes," he said. "Quite a different thing than what I was thinking. Yeah, we can get that on the calendar."

Kari stared across the road and sipped her coffee, clearly disgusted.

"You think you're ever going to settle down, Uncle Chris?" I asked.

He gave me a side-eye and quickly looked away. A silence grew, and internal alarms sounded as I realized I may have hit a sore subject. I scrambled to think of something to say to let him off the hook, but he replied before I came up with anything.

He shook his head. "Naw. One time long ago, I had my chance. Us O'Neil's are one woman kind of men. Just look at your dad. Or Oscar."

His answer had me gobsmacked in a couple of different ways. I worked my mouth, trying to respond but my brain was trucking a million miles a second. He'd once been in love? What had happened? And he brought up Oscar! Was I making progress?

"What happened?" was the question I finally settled on. I peeped at him over my cup.

His jaw worked, and I could see he was trying to control his emotions. But his voice was lighthearted, even dismissive. "Same experience as a million others. Wrong person, wrong time." I swear, as he said that, he flushed and looked guilty.

The question clearly rattled him, because he stood up, ready to make his get-away. "Anyway, that's a story for another day. Right now, I've got some phone calls to make." He brushed his hands on his pants after shoving in the last bite of doughnut.

Kari got ready as well. Ever the mom, she gathered up all the spare napkins and garbage and carried them to the can.

Uncle Chris headed out before us. As I followed, I couldn't help but wonder, who was this mystery woman he'd once loved? These O'Neil men were full of secrets.

Back at the office, the three of us split to our work spaces. I revamped the Johnson's house listing to include in bold print **—Potential interested parties must be represented by a licensed agent.** Uncle Chris made sure the security team was in place at the property and by noon, they had already chased off a few more looky-lous. He'd also booked a scuba recovery team, due out tomorrow.

The word must have gotten out, because the calls asking for showings of the Johnson place dried up to nothing. The rest of my day was spent answering emails. As I expected, not one person who had been there this morning sent in an offer.

Well, that's just my luck. I sighed. I felt like I was going to be saddled with the lake listing forever. As if to highlight my bad luck, I received a text from Mrs. Crawford reminding me of dinner that night.

I stared at the text as a heavy feeling of dread crawled over me. *Why did I say yes?*

Kari must have heard me groan because she glanced over from her computer screen, "What's going on? More trouble at the Johnson's place?"

I winced, one eye open, one eye squinched. "No. Even better. I have a blind date tonight."

"Oooh," Kari said, nodding sympathetically. "Well, that could be fun. Who roped you in?"

"My landlord."

"You'll have a good time, you'll see." There was a moment of silence as she typed away at on her keyboard. Then she tapped her chin as if a thought had just occurred to her. "You know, I have a great person you might like to meet. He's tall, dark, and handsome, and recently single."

I smiled even as I internally whimpered. "Thanks for the thought. I'll let you know."

"We'll figure a fun way for you two to meet," she promised with a wink.

I weakly smiled back and finished my paperwork.

The work day ended early with another storm blowing in. I drove home with the mindset of getting into a hot bath and doing a little investigating before heading out to dinner.

Normally, I wasn't a bath girl. But this house had one of my favorite things, a claw-foot tub. It made me investigate a whole new world of bath bombs, and I was having a blast with them.

As I was leaving town, I passed Fast Lanes car dealership. They had a car sitting out front that made me suck in my breath. A Plum Crazy Purple 1970 Dodge Challenger.

I'd always loved hot rods, especially after having a boyfriend in high school who drove a Dodge Dart. There was a season where we went to every muscle car show, and I lived and breathed everything from posi traction to Hemi engines.

I'd wanted my own, except Dad did the whole, "over my dead body" routine, and then college came along with student loans and effectively killed that whole dream. I squeezed the steering wheel and sighed. Maybe someday.

Once, home I headed straight for the bathroom, filled up the tub with steaming water, and dropped in a lavender stress-reliever. I figured that tonight I needed all the help I could get.

A few minutes later I was in the tub, my back supported by a little blow-up air pillow, with my phone on a tray before me. Lavender scented steam filled the room.

Okay, time to get back to business. I wiggled my toes in the hot water and checked Trek's World to see if I'd received any answering messages from GettingStamped.

There was nothing. Not even an indication to show if he'd read what I'd sent. Of course, GettingStamped could be a woman. Heck, it could be a ten-year-old kid, for all I knew.

That made me wonder if he used his name elsewhere. I typed in GettingStamped in the search engine to see what it brought up.

It did bring up another forum. It was like the first one I'd found about unsolved riddles. Only this one said, Gamer Easter Eggs revealed.

The front page blew my mind. The title said, "Sacred Sword Riddle Solved?"

I clicked it and eagerly read.

*Hey guys, word on the street says there will be a scuba extraction at the lake tomorrow at noon. Are you going to be there?*

At the bottom were comments, people saying things like, "The house fits since it once belonged to Ava Summers, the author of the riddle. Her dad owned the Johnson house."

"Where is it again? Brookfield?"

"I'm totally going to be there!"

"I was there today. None of us found anything. I'm telling you, this is a dead end."

GettingStamped had posted, "It's there, folks!"

Was the sword there or was it not? I couldn't wait until tomorrow. My gosh, what if the divers brought up an ancient sword? What would that even be worth? Millions, probably. Definitely more money than I could imagine. I wondered if the owners would be driving down from New York. Was it going to be another zoo scene like today? There was a security team there, but would that be enough?

Excitement zinged through me as I finally realized what tomorrow might bring. Then, I glanced at the clock, and the euphoric feeling rushed away faster than the water down the drain.

It was nearly time for my date.

I climbed out and was wrapping a towel around me when another thought jumped in my mind. I might know a way I could track GettingStamped down, after all.

I clicked back to Trek's World and typed in his name to see what else he posted. The posts were sparse and mostly located in the role-playing forum. I scanned through them, which consisted mostly of gamer talk and questions.

One of his posts stopped me right away. It said, "Hey, follow me on youtube if you want to see more of my action."

*Well, now. This was exciting.* Was I about to identify who GettingStamped really was? I went to the video site and pasted his name in the search bar. The results made me grin.

He had his own channel.

Of course, anyone could get a channel, so I wasn't sure how big of a deal it was. But there were thirty-two videos listed under his name.

I clicked the first one. I was a little dismayed when I saw it was over an hour long. That was going to be a lot of watching.

The video opened with some cheesy graphics that signified it was definitely produced by an amateur. The next scene was of a role-play game on the video screen. There was no sign of him, but I could hear that he was a man by the narration.

I watched for a few minutes. His comments were very relevant to the game, mostly, "Ha! See that?" His videos seemed to be just about him playing the game and showing people how it was done.

It was about as interesting as watching paint dry, but then again, I didn't play those games. I'm sure someone out there appreciated it.

I checked to see how many times the video had been viewed. Nearly all were in the hundreds, which was a low amount. I clicked through a few of the comments and didn't see anything of interest, mostly just of spam advertising other videos.

There was one though, that said, "I knew I'd find you here." The commenter was anonymous.

Huh. That's interesting.

It was then I realized I had less than twenty minutes to get ready for dinner. Quickly, I brushed my hair, hoping to make it look decent.

Who was I kidding? At this point, I needed a miracle.

# CHAPTER 13

I was late, but finally arrived at Mrs. Crawford's house, feeling like something the cat dragged in. I got out of the car and brushed down my skirt. I couldn't believe I was so nervous. This was ridiculous. *I'm fine. I'm completely in control.*

I walked up the stairs, suddenly struck with the fear that I might have sweated through my shirt. The imagined wet stains made me groan, and I nearly turned back around. To be honest I might have, except right then the front door opened, bathing me in warm light.

"Stella, is that you dear?" Mrs. Crawford stood in the doorway. As always, she was dressed impeccably. Tonight she wore white silk pants and a long flowing shirt. Her characteristic chunky necklace was blue tonight. "I thought I heard you pull up. Come in! We were just talking about you."

Talking about me? This just keeps getting better and better. I mustered up a fake smile. Behind her I could see the dark silhouetted form of a man.

"Hi, guys," I said, trying to keep my voice from wavering. "I'm sorry I'm late. Traffic...." It took every ounce of muscle control to continue up the stairs and work my face to try to appear friendly. That was no easy feat, by the way. My face was famous for showing everything I was thinking, and was also known as the great betrayer.

The scent of simmering chicken greeted me as I got closer to the door. Mrs. Crawford held out a hand.

"You look lovely, dear," she said with a warm smile and a gentle squeeze.

I swallowed hard and turned to face the blind date she'd set me up with.

"This is David," she said, indicating the shadowed man with a sweep of her hand.

David stepped forward, dressed as though he'd just walked out of a library or maybe a classroom teaching statistic mathematics. His hair was short, possibly because it was thinning. He was thin himself, with pale skin and a long sharp nose. He reached out to shake, making me note his lanky arms.

To be honest, I was half-offended that Mrs. Crawford thought I would be compatible with him. I could already picture a long evening ahead, filled with nervous clearing of his throat and claustrophobic silences.

"Stella," he said. "It's nice to meet you."

Whoa. His voice took me off guard. It was full-bodied and deep. And was that...an accent? I shook his hand and gave him a second look. His gray eyes held mine in confidence and he gave me a small smile.

"Nice to meet you. I've heard nothing but good things." I said in return.

"Likewise," he answered, releasing me.

"Well, now, isn't this nice." Mrs. Crawford slowly scooted us in further so she could shut the door. "Let's go sit for a minute and have a glass of wine."

Wine. Wine would probably help. We followed her into the living room, with its two armchairs and long couch upholstered in expensive white fabric. Every inch of the walls were covered in framed art and golden do-dads displayed on scattered curio shelves.

She pointed to the wine credenza. "David, would you do the honors?" Gracefully, she sat in one of the armchairs and brushed a long brown curl from her shoulder.

"Absolutely," he said and sprang in that direction. Carefully, he uncorked the bottle from where he'd retrieved it from the ice bucket, and poured three glasses.

I'd chosen the other armchair and smiled as he brought me my glass. He settled on the couch across from me.

The dreadful silence began. Hurriedly, I took a sip and stared into the fireplace flames.

"So, David. You were saying," Mrs. Crawford prompted.

"Oh!" he scooted to the edge of the sofa and faced me. "I was in the middle of explaining how I got my doctorate in statistics."

Figures. I knew it.

"Anyway, to treat myself, I ended up traveling around Europe for several months."

"Really!" I said.

"Yeah, it's been a lot of fun. Ireland was one of my favorite countries."

"I want to take a trip to Ireland but it will be a while yet before I can." I noticed I was leaning forward myself, and subtly scooted back in my chair.

"Oh, you never know. Maybe after your first sale." Mrs. Crawford said, tapping her foot. And then to David, "Stella, here, is a realtor."

I cringed at how boring that sounded. And I thought a doctorate in Statistics was bad.

His eyebrows raised and he nodded as though fascinated. "I bet you meet some characters in the business, hmm?"

I nodded. "You can't even imagine. In fact, the latest one I've met is dead."

He'd just taken a sip and sputtered in his glass. "Dead?" he managed to ask after a moment.

"Yes. Most likely murdered," Mrs. Crawford volunteered for me.

"Well now," he shook his head. "Seems like there's more to that job description than meets the eye."

I quickly filled him in on what had happened the other day.

"So, any suspects?" he asked.

"The police are looking into the man's neighbor. Roy Merlock is his name. They've had a rivalry that's extended through the generations. Mostly arguing over property lines and such."

"Hmm, you think Roy killed him in the lake?"

I tried to picture the two old men grappling in the water until Roy finally struck the fatal blow. It just didn't make sense to me. I shook my head. "But Roy's been heard to make threats, and he has that old family grudge so..." I trailed off.

"You think he hired someone to do it?"

Now there's a thought I hadn't considered. "Maybe." I nodded. "That would make more sense."

"Now what about clues. Did you find anything by the lake? Maybe garbage, or something?" David swirled the remainder of wine in his glass.

Well, of course I'd found the flippers and the note, but when he asked that it reminded me of the Dr. Pepper can I'd seen.

"I found a pop can. But there were a lot of cops on the scene when they recovered his body."

His eyebrows went up like he had an Aha moment. "Statistically, it was unlikely a rescue attendant of any sort would be drinking a soda and then tossing the trash to the ground, especially at a murder scene. I think you may have found yourself a real clue."

I took a sip, thinking.

"So, where are you from, originally?" he asked, changing the subject.

"Me? Oh, I was actually born here, but I grew up in the northwest."

"Really? And what part?"

"Just outside Seattle. At the base of the Cascades."

"It's beautiful out there," David noted.

I agreed. "But with your travels, you must see much prettier landscape."

"Oh, no. I love and appreciate every part I'm fortunate enough to visit. But give me the USA. It's a gorgeous country. Never underestimate what's familiar."

"Have you been to Egypt?" Mrs. Crawford asked in that cool tone of hers.

"I have. One day I plan to go to Israel. I'd loved to see it."

Excitement curled in my chest. "Me too! The history is amazing." Being able to join the conversation about a foreign country made me feel so cosmopolitan.

We talked for a while and then eventually moved into the dining room. So far, it really wasn't so bad. David and I might not be a match made in heaven, but at least I was back in the saddle again. And he was a nice guy. Quiet, a little nerdy, but nice. The chicken fricassee was wonderful, and I laughed more than I'd laughed in a long time. I also went home much later than I'd planned. Which is to say, it was quite a nice night.

# CHAPTER 14

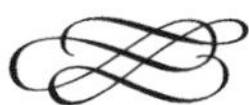

The next morning started with a ton of regrets that I'd chosen to leave the dinner party so late, when the alarm ripped me from my warm bed. Somewhere in the middle of the second glass of wine, I'd forgotten I needed to be up early.

Today was a big day at the Johnson place. In just a few hours, we'd finally learn the secrets under the lake.

I hurried to brush my teeth and dress, then grabbed a granola bar and a travel mug of coffee, and I was on my way. I thought about the clues I knew so far, the flippers, the Dr. Pepper can, the note with the poem on it, the book written by Ava Summers, the daughter of the original owner—that would make her Lenny's grandma?— and the scuba tank sticker.

I couldn't wait to find out what was discovered. I wasn't alone. The Johnson's driveway was crowded with cars. I'd expected a lot of buzz, but I was surprised to see two local news vans there. Of course, they would come. This was quite the scoop, especially for this little town. If the sword were unearthed, it would make a huge ripple in the historical community at large.

I recognized one of the reporters. She was in her early twenties, blonde, beautiful, although struggling at the moment with the wind whipping her hair in her face. She spat it out and yelled at her camera guy to find a better spot for the shoot.

"Where do you want me to go?" he asked. "The lake's right behind you." His forehead wrinkled with irritation although his voice was calm. It sounded like a normal interaction for them.

"Brian! I don't care where we are. Just get me out of the mud and wind!"

"And, we're live, in three...two...one," he calmly counted down, ignoring her outburst.

Like a lightbulb, she switched from the petulant frown to a million-dollar smile. "Hello, folks! We're here live today, despite the wind"—she gave a tinkling laugh—"to discover what secrets the Johnson Lake holds under its murky surface.

It's been rumored to be the answer to an eighty-year-old riddle, stating an ancient sword is hidden beneath this muddy surface."

Here Brian lifted the camera and slowly panned the water's surface.

"We're told," the reporter continued, "That beneath the lake is a professional scuba diving team, who are searching the ruins of a house long forgotten beneath the surface. Any minute now, we expect to hear some news."

"And cut!" yelled the cameraman.

Immediately the reporter's smile fell. "Now can you get me out of this cow field?"

I glanced down and saw her nice, expensive boots were indeed covered in mud. My own feet were stuffed into a pair of cheap rain boots I'd purchased specifically for walking out to the mailbox at my rental home.

I left her and squelched through the mud in a search for Uncle Chris, and soon found him standing with what looked like a member of the scuba team by the lake's shore. There was a tent covering some equipment and electrical wires strung from the house over there. I didn't continue my trek, not wanting to disturb them.

Someone grabbed my arm and I spun with surprise, and then smiled at Kari.

"Exciting day!" she exclaimed, her blonde hair covered with a beanie, sporting a huge fake-fur pompom. "Looks like half the town is here to see what they're going to find." She lowered her voice and pulled me in closer. "Including Roy Merlock."

"What?" I asked. "Where is he?"

She lifted her eyes and cut them to the left. I followed the gaze to see an old man standing near a stump, his hands shoved deep in his pockets, and a stocking cap pulled low on his forehead.

"Wow, amazing that he'd even show his face," I whispered.

"Especially since he's a suspect for murder," Kari added. She cooly glanced at him again and then turned back to the lake.

"What do you think they'll find? You think the sword is really down there?" I asked. The wind was tearing at my hair, too. I knotted it as best as I could and pulled up the hood on my jacket.

"I wouldn't be surprised if they pulled out a purple kangaroo, at this point. What a crazy ride this has been. And your first listing, too!"

I nodded, my attention caught by two men in their early

twenties. Both of them were walking up to Roy on the hill. Roy nodded at them, but otherwise was expressionless.

"What?" asked Kari, catching a glimpse of my face.

"Roy has friends," I said, dipping my head in his direction.

She casually glanced over. "One of those guys works at Roy's sport shop. He does repairs on the bikes."

"Really?" I said, squinting at him. He had a cut on his cheek. "He looks awful similar to the guy that I chased off this property the other day."

"Oh, really! Do you recognize the other guy he's with?"

I squinted harder and she nudged me. "Don't stare!" she warned.

"How am I supposed to tell if I've seen him before or not if I don't stare?" I replied. Still, I turned my head, because, right when Kari warned me, the man had glanced in my direction as if he felt my eyes on him.

"Good one," Kari mumbled. "He saw us."

"That means you were looking too," I whispered back. "And no, I don't recognize him. But that doesn't mean he wasn't here. There was a huge group by the lake that disappeared when the cops showed up."

"Well, that's Roy's son, Jay. He's our mailman," she noted.

It really was turning into a town reunion. "Did I tell you that I found a pair of swim fins in the house?"

"No, but your uncle did. He showed me the picture and what caught my eye was the name Regional. That's a brand carried by Laughing Gull Sport Shop."

I frowned for a second. "Well, it seems like a lot of places probably carry the same brand."

She shrugged. "Well, you'd think so. But when I told Joe, he said they were hard to get and that was one of the only places he knew of that still had them. Joe's big on fishing so he knows that kind of stuff."

I nodded, distracted. There was some action happening out in the water. A rowboat was moving fast to the middle of the lake. Everyone watched as the tension built. I texted Uncle Chris. **—Any news?**

I could see him fish his phone from his pocket. He read the text and then typed.**—Not yet. You coming?**

I texted back. **—I'm by the house next to Kari.**

He slowly spun in the house's direction, searching for me. When he found me, he raised his hand and I raised mine back.

We didn't have time for more than that because the crowd at the bank shouted and cheered. Two heads poked above the water's surface like seals. The rowboat moved towards them.

The newscaster turned on her reporting voice, "As you can see, the diver's have returned from their search. This is very exciting!"

Speculations flew up and down the beach. I heard snippets. "He's got something, did you see it?"

"I knew it!"

"Naw, he's moving too slow. He doesn't have anything."

The answer came nonverbally. One of the divers looked toward the tent. Bobbing up and down as he tread water, he made a thumbs down.

A collective groan echoed around us as we all heaved a disappointed sigh. It didn't matter what the divers were going to say to the reporter, it was obvious they'd found nothing.

"Well, there goes our town's future claim to fame," Kari said, bouncing in place to warm her legs. "We were *this* close to being the realty that sold the property where an ancient artifact was found. I knew it was nothing but an old wives' tale."

"Someone died because of that tale," I reminded her. After a second, I realized, "and this just could be proof that it was found during his dive after all."

She raised her eyebrows. "So, you think Lenny really found something, then."

"Statistically, it's possible," I said, half prompted by David.

"So it could have been him, after all," she said, glancing at Roy.

I wrinkled my nose as I considered the old man. "It's hard to picture him diving, let alone wrestling and stabbing someone to death in the water."

"What are you talking about?" Kari asked. "Just because you're retired, doesn't mean you can't do things. Half this society's advancements and treasures have come from people who had retired."

Suitably scolded, I nodded. "You're right."

"You better believe I'm right. He could be a killer if he wants to," she nodded emphatically.

"I'm sure that's every retiree's goal," I teased.

"Honey, by that age, I'm sure you're done taking crap and you've started to realize you wouldn't serve that long of a sentence in prison anyway."

I rolled my eyes as we started to walk toward Uncle Chris, joining a crowd of people who were heading the same way, like a human amoeba.

"Anyway, it appears we're back to business as usual. You shouldn't have any more trouble here with people trespassing now that they've debunked the myth." She clapped me on my shoulder. "Let's get this place sold!"

# CHAPTER 15

The divers did give an interview. The blonde reporter held the mic to their mouths and nodded empathetically with a concerned pout to her lips.

The first diver said that from what he could tell, the house hadn't been disturbed since soon after it had originally flooded. In fact, he said, there was no way into the building without some major excavating because the structure had collapsed.

More groans met his statement. The human amoeba that we were, slowly shifted back to the cars, even while the divers were still being interviewed. It was a disappointing end to the morning for all of us, even though this let me off the hook as far as a house sale going through.

I left Uncle Chris still talking with the divers and drove back to town. I figured I'd see him later in the office.

I passed the Fast Lanes car dealership again, and spotted the purple Challenger that had first caught my eye. It would be fun just to take it for a test drive. I pictured myself sitting behind the wheel, windows down, the rumble of the engine as I got ready to take off. And purple too! One of my favorite colors. She was beautiful.

Yep. I was going to do it. I was going to at least take it for a spin. And, if I ever sold a house, I'd start socking some money away.

Dad might not like it but I'm sure Uncle Chris would approve.

Thinking of Uncle Chris reminded me of our conversation where he'd brought up Oscar. It started awkward, with his mention of some secret woman he'd once loved. I'd really love to get to the bottom of that story. What type of woman would have fallen for him? He was so rough around the edges, kind of a boozer, definitely out of shape.

However, if it had been back in his car racing days, I could see the attraction. Fast cars, the excitement of winning, the camaraderie and respect of the fellow drivers. He probably had the pick of the groupies.

It was sad that Uncle Chris had never fallen in love again.

But the important part was that he'd also commented about how all the O'Neils were one-woman men. The fact that he was finding even a tiny bit of common ground with his dad made me feel like I was making progress in bringing this family a step closer toward reconciliation.

Oscar was quite the character. Gruff and grouchy, but I could already sense the soft interior he kept hidden inside. Despite my reservations, I was starting to trust him. I knew there was another side to the story; Dad's side, Uncle Chris's side, and Oscar's side. I had a feeling they weren't so different, after all.

It was noon now. After everything that'd happened—or hadn't happen—this morning, I really wanted to talk to Oscar and get his view. I had some time. Maybe I could stop by.

I figured, since I was coming unannounced, I'd better get a peace offering first.

I drove to Darcy's Doughnuts and walked inside to their sugary heaven-scented haven. It was a hard choice, but I finally picked out a half dozen that I thought he'd like, including a cherry turnover. Thus armed with goodies, stomach growling, I headed for Baker Street.

Nerves tickled my backbone as I turned down the driveway and parked the car. I was half on the edge of thinking this was the dumbest idea ever, and hoped he would be okay with me just showing up. I walked up to the door. A comforting, homey scent wrapped around me.... spaghetti.

My mouth watered. I shuffled the box of doughnuts to my other hand and, after hesitating for a second, knocked on the door.

Barking welcomed me in the form of a puffy yellow tornado as Peanut raced down the hallway. *Bear,* I mentally corrected myself, remembering what Oscar called her.

My pale face reflecting in the window appeared like I was in pain. It was obvious I'd had too little sleep and was steeped in disappointment. I smiled, and the image only grew worse, a strange grimace, like strings were pulling up the corners of my lips. Good grief, I looked like a puppet straight out of the movie, Dark Crystal. I loved the movie, but not enough to be a character.

While I was thinking all of this, I realized I was making faces at Oscar. He was on the other side of the glass about to open the door. I flushed and glanced down, and then back up and tried to smile again.

"Well, now. What do I owe the pleasure of this visit?" Oscar said, as he opened the door. The scent of spicy meatballs and garlic rolled out like a red carpet.

"Hi." I offered out the box. "I was at the bakery and thought of you."

He blinked as he stared at the box. "What's this?"

I was tempted to make a smart remark, tell him it was a box of crickets or something, but I couldn't. We just weren't there yet.

However, if he offered me a plate of spaghetti with a few meatballs, I'd consider us family bonded forever.

"Pastries," I said. "Chocolate eclair and a cherry turnover." I shook the box lightly, hoping it would tempt him.

"Mmm," he said. "One of those moments, huh? Well, I've never been one to say no to a doughnut. Come on in."

I entered the house, dancing around Peanut in an attempt to not step on her paws or trip over her body which seemed attracted to my feet like a magnet.

"One of those moments?" I asked, repeating what he'd said.

He didn't answer, instead he shuffled into the kitchen. He had on the same plaid slippers, and baggy jeans as I last saw on him. But this time he'd snazzed it up with a blue-checked shirt and a pair of red suspenders.

Bubbling on the stove was the spaghetti sauce that had lured me in, along with a pot of noodles. There was even a frying pan in the sink where I detected the evidence of pan-fried meatballs that were presumably now in the sauce.

I was no match for such deliciousness. My mouth watered as I set the box down and picked up Peanut.

"Bear, missed you," Oscar said in his gruff voice. He used a fork to fish out a noodle and tested it by throwing it against the wall.

He nodded when it stuck. "Dinner's ready." He glanced at me over the tops of his glasses. "And you're just in time."

Okay, this was getting weird. It was almost as if he had expected me.

He whistled as he got out a strainer and drained the noodles. His whistle was light and at the same time soothing. He returned the noodles to the pot and stuck in a pair of tongs. To the sauce, he added a ladle.

"Plates are over there," he nodded. "I'm not dishing you up."

I set down the dog, who scampered off, washed my hands in the sink and then got a plate. It was white with tiny goldenrod flowers circling the edge. Oscar scooped sauce over his noodles. I was pleased to see there were meatballs.

He got me a glass of water while I dished myself up. Then we sat across one another for our second meal together.

I was dying to ask him what he meant when I came in. He bowed his head for a moment, so I held my tongue. Finally, as he spooled up noodles, I prodded him with the question again. "What did you mean, one of those moments?"

"A talking moment. When something's really weighing on your heart. You bring doughnuts, I know it's a big weight."

His words hit hard, in a scary place. This was eerily close to what I'd been thinking. He couldn't know me that fast, could he? I twisted my fork in the pasta. There was no sound for a few moments other than the clink of our silverware against the plates.

I couldn't stand it any more. "How did you know?"

"How did I know? How did I know what? That you would be showing up? Every Tom, Dick, and Harry has been playing that interview from the diver up there at the Johnson's place. How'd I know it'd weigh heavy on you? Because I know you want to get to the bottom of what happened to Lenny Johnson. How did I know you'd show up here, having a moment?" He glanced at me then, and then his jaw jumped as though he were clenching his teeth. As if he couldn't take it, he poured his attention back into the spaghetti before him. "Because you're like your dad. And you're like your grandma. You keep words locked inside of your head that need a sounding board in order to come out."

I blew out my cheeks, realizing how true his statement was. And I realized I had so many things to ask. Suddenly, I could barely breathe as they all bubbled to get out, like a herd of cattle rushing a tiny gate. Did Oscar ever try to contact my dad? Did he miss me? Did he know about my great great grandmother's letters? So many things.

"Okay...I guess I do have a question for you," I murmured slowly. The only way I was going to get answers was to go for it. I might as well take the plunge.

Oscar raised his eyebrows but didn't say anything. I think he was slightly concerned at what might pop out of my mouth, because he cut his meatball with a little extra gusto.

I twisted the napkin on my lap then saw what I did with it and tried to unfold it.

He cleared his throat. "You nervous? Ask away."

Uh. I didn't know how to answer that. "Mm, a little."

"Well, I won't bite. At least not without my good denture glue."

I choked back an unexpected laugh. My emotions were all over the place, all of a sudden. Nerves like wet noodles, I tell you. Why was I so scared of a man whose body had been bent by age and wore glasses thick enough to start fires if left in the direct sunlight?

Because of what my dad had told me.

Oscar watched me now, his fork held in mid-air. It was as if he could read my mind. He caught my eye and smiled, and lowered his fork. Slowly, he twirled the noodles. "My grandmother always told me you couldn't cry in the rain. It wastes water."

I swallowed hard, having read that very quote in her letters. "What do you think that meant?"

"It means what it needs to mean at the time," he said. "You tell me."

"Were you close to your grandma?" I asked.

"She was an amazing woman. She died much too young."

"Did she get a chance to meet your wife?" I asked, referring to my grandma.

"No. But she would have loved her."

"What was Grandma like?" There, I'd asked the big kahuna. Would he be able to tell me?

His head dropped, and I was horrified to see his hand tremble. He set down his fork and his hands folded into one another. After a moment, he swallowed hard to compose himself. "Your grandmother—" His voice cracked and he stopped. He cleared his throat and began again. "Your grandmother was a saint. She raised two boys nearly alone, and was always there for me. I wasn't the best father. My job took me away from the family time and time again. I loved hunting those bad guys. It's what I did. It's what I was good at. But it was a huge sacrifice for her. The world will never know what she gave."

"Is that why..." I hesitated, scared to offend him. "Is that why my dad and Uncle Chris are so angry with you?"

"Your grandma asked me to quit many times. But it was my identity. It was all I knew. I couldn't do it. They never forgave me."

"I'm sorry," I said. The atmosphere felt heavy. I waited, not sure of what to say next.

"You know, I saw you in track," he said simply.

My jaw dropped. "What?"

"You know, your races. Things you did in school."

I didn't know what to say. I kind of felt like I'd just been swept up into the Twilight zone. He'd slammed the brakes and turned the conversation around so fast, I was reeling.

"You saw me?"

"Yeah. I kept tabs on you guys when you were in Washington. Tried to always keep out of sight. You did well. I was proud."

"I can't believe you were there." Maybe I should have been

freaked out, but instead I felt shame. Tears stung my eyes and I blotted them with my napkin. He didn't know how I'd failed in college. I couldn't tell him.

"Why didn't you say anything?" I said.

"What could I say? Your dad didn't want anything to do with me. He was trying to protect you from me." He stopped abruptly and glanced around. "Peanut!" he bellowed. I was surprised he didn't mess around with calling her Bear. He must need her fuzziness right away.

The dog came running, her little nails scrabbling against the hard wood floor. She danced on her hind legs until he lifted her up. His arthritic hand rested on her head.

"I did send flowers," he said. "Three of them every Valentine's Day."

I covered my mouth. "That was you?"

Our school did single rose deliveries for Valentine's Day. Students and parents ordered them for each other. I'd always get four and assumed they were all from my dad.

I stared at my plate, my eyes filling with tears. Hurriedly, I dabbed at them with my destroyed napkin. I was overwhelmed to know the effort he'd made, to know he'd even cared. "Thank you."

"I did what I could. I was proud of you."

I couldn't take it any more. "Please don't say that."

"What? What do you mean?"

"I mean, I was really nothing to be proud of." I laughed, feeling sardonic. "When I arrived at college, I quickly realized I was nothing special."

He rolled his eyes. "Will you knock it off."

"What?" Here I was coming clean with this gut wrenching truth, and he was eyeballing me like I was being prissy over not getting designer shoes.

"I mean, you need to quit feeling sorry for yourself." He forked a mouthful of spaghetti in and chewed.

"I'm not! It's something serious that I've really had to come to terms with."

He shook his head. "You're trying to wrap up a bad feeling in a smart package, but no matter the paper, it's pouting through and through. Your problem is that you hooked your value on an action. Listen sharp, girlie. There's always going to be someone who's better, prettier, smarter, and faster, but it doesn't devalue what you can do. Don't you know that you have to love yourself enough to appreciate when you give your very best?"

My mouth opened, and shut, and then opened again. I'm sure I looked like a goldfish greedily chasing after fish flakes. I hadn't thought of it that way, and I honestly was kind of stunned.

I had no idea where I'd learned that if you weren't the best, you were nothing. I thought back to Dad, but he'd never told me that. In fact, he'd cheered just as loudly at my last race, as my first.

A lump grew in my throat at the thought of Dad. Memories of how he'd taken care of me flashed through my head. He wasn't perfect, but he was the perfect dad for me. "You're right, I know you are. Dad did try to teach me that. I'm not sure why it didn't stick. I'll try to hang on to that truth now." I spun my fork in the noodles, playing with them. "You know, Dad may not like to hear it, but his parenting is partially to your credit. He *is* half you."

"Well, he got all my good stuff then." Oscar grinned.

"Hey, what about Uncle Chris?" I smiled back, happy to feel the mood lightening.

He rolled his eyes. "Now that boy is a pancake short of a Denny's breakfast meal."

I choked on a noodle and laughed. "He's funny, but he's been really helpful getting me settled here." I cut a meatball and speared half. "I think he might be open to talking with you. I actually think he would like that."

Oscar scratched Peanut's ears. "No rush."

I raised an eyebrow. "I don't know about that. If you want to talk with him, we don't have a whole lot of time to waste."

"You calling me old, young lady?"

I shrugged. "If the cane fits."

There was silence as a response. I glanced over, terrified that my joke had gone to far. I was surprised to see his eyes shut. A slow wheeze came out. I realized it was a laugh.

I smiled too, and stuffed another bite into my mouth. Dang, these meatballs were good.

"Now, what's going on with this house murder of yours?" Oscar said.

I finished chewing and wiped my mouth. "Well, my biggest problem is that they didn't find a motive for Lenny to be murdered. And it really struck me as odd that Roy Merlock would be there. I mean... if it's true he killed Lenny. Why would he show up if he'd known the sword wasn't there?" I took a sip of water and then asked, "You said you knew Lenny. How did you know him?"

"I met him at the barber shop." Oscar rubbed his hand over Peanut's ear, cupping them like little pony tails. He didn't have a lot of hair on his own head, and eyed me as if daring me to say something about it. "I know what you're thinking.

We'd play checkers. I'd lose. I'd have to buy him a Dr. Pepper."

*Wait, what?* "You bought him a soda?"

"Dr. Pepper. The man was addicted to them."

I covered my face with my hands. Lenny must have brought the soda with him before he dived and chucked the can. There went one of my clues.

"I give up," I muffled.

"What?"

"I said—" I lowered my hands, filled with exasperation.

"I know what you said." Oscar's eyebrows lowered. Suddenly, he appeared quite fierce. "I don't want to hear those words from your mouth, again. You're no quitter. You're an O'Neil. I've watched you race kids three years older than you, with legs twice as long. And you won more than you lost. You got straight *A*s, you put yourself through college. You are amazing, and you don't give up. Ever." He cleared his throat and his voice softened. "Give yourself some breathing room and some time to think. I believe in you, young lady." He stared at me some more, before going back to spooling his spaghetti. "And don't think for one second I've gone soft. That cherry turnover is mine."

## CHAPTER 16

I left Oscar's house considerably fortified, both in the stomach region and my heart. For the first time since relocating from Seattle, I was convinced it had been the right move for me, and I was more determined than ever to repair the broken bridge between Oscar and his sons.

Speaking of his sons, I thought of those swim fins. Uncle Chris had said he knew someone on the police force. I wondered if he'd received any information about them.

Before I left the driveway, I sent a quick text. —**Hey, Uncle Chris. Any news on the flippers?**

He answered back. —**Only that Roy insists they're not from his shop. But you left a little early. The divers did find a piece of jewelry sitting on the**

**shore. We all walked past it a million times. It was a lucky find.**

**—Really? What is it? Can you send me a picture?**

**—Probably just some costume jewelry. But it's still interesting.**

A minute later, a photo appeared. The jewelry piece was a round circle and black with tarnish. Interesting. I'd check it out later. Still feeling full of contentment, I started the car and drove home.

I knew the police had Roy Merlock under a microscope, but was it possible there was something they were missing? He denied the flippers came from his shop. But what about the sticker on the air tank? And I heard the murderer always returns to the scene of the crime. He *had* been there at the lake this morning.

After arriving at the house, I tossed my keys on the counter, and immediately headed for my computer. My mind was ramped up and I wanted to dig into this. I settled into my chair and opened a search engine, and then typed in the brand name of the flippers.

The first thing I discovered was that Kari's husband was right. It was a specialty brand. And not only that, but the business had gone under last year. Every link I clicked showed them to be out of stock, with the exception of eBay. Could the owner of the flippers have ordered them from eBay and, if so, how could that person be tracked down? I chewed my lip, wondering if it was possible. I rubbed my temples, trying not to be discouraged.

But wait! Who said the swim fins were new? Maybe the person had owned them for a few years already.

Okay, back up. I thought this person had to be friends with Old Man Lenny. Another theory I couldn't rule out was that it was someone who had snuck up on him. That was still a theory I couldn't rule out. But how would the person have known that Lenny would be at the lake?

I tried to picture it. The first scenario, two friends who ended in a death struggle. The second, an enemy who followed Lenny into the lake and took him out.

Honestly, the first scenario gave me the shivers. What kind of evil person would befriend someone and then do that?

So, how does Roy fit into this scenario? He'd definitely be the enemy. It was obvious he had all the equipment. But how would he know Lenny was going to be there that morning?

So many questions.

I grabbed my phone and scrolled to the picture of the

pendant Uncle Chris had sent. Where did it come from? Was it just some piece of costume jewelry?

Good questions for the search engine. I typed in 19th century circular jewelry pendants, trying to hit the time-line when the original homestead was built.

It brought up an extensive list of earrings, hat pins, and pendants. I scrolled through the images, hunting for anything remotely similar to the picture. Silver items were the most popular, with the occasional gold piece. There were even a few made from copper and nickel.

The pendant in the picture was tarnished to the point I couldn't tell the type of metal it was, nor make out the design on the front. If I squinted, it looked like a face. Or an elephant. *Hmmm.*

I wondered, was it only silver metal that tarnished? I typed that question in and hit search. The spinning thing told me it was thinking. I'm sure whoever developed the software meant that symbol to be comforting, but it irritated me.

Spin, spin, spin. This was getting me nowhere fast except frustrated. I decided to get myself a snack and a breather. One plate of cinnamon toast and a mug of peppermint tea coming up. When I came back with my plate, I saw the computer had decided to answer. I was surprised to learn quite a few metals aged with a patina.

I stuffed a corner of the toast in my mouth and chewed, then typed "pendants with faces."

A million results showed up. This was worse than a needle in a haystack. I shoved my keyboard away, half-feeling like throwing it.

My gaze caught the sight of the dangling wallpaper.

Yes, ma'am. Today was the day. I stalked over there, fueled with irritation that I hadn't been able to find the answers to even one thing I'd searched for. Seriously, what good was technology if it always gave me a million choices? I reached for the piece of wallpaper. And who would do roses for an entire house, anyway? I liked the flower as much as the next person, but every square inch?

"I'm tired of not being able to find Old Man Lenny's killer." I yanked. It tore in the most satisfying way. "I'm tired of not being able to find one single solid lead on any of the clues I've found." I yanked harder. The strip tore to the floor with a satisfying *Thwap*!

As I wobbled it up, my eyebrows raised. There, in the very bottom corner of the wall, near the stair tread, was some writing. A poem of some sort. I was about sick of poems, but this one seemed different.

It was a children's poem.

*Red and Yellow, loves a fellow. On December of this year, Gaila was here.*

Gaila, huh? The block print was sloppy, but it still had careful, measured strokes that called back to innocence. I knew where I'd seen that kind of writing before. My friend's daughter had given me a homemade going-away card when I'd left Washington last year. It had about made me cry. There were two crayoned snowmen encircled in carefully printed rainbow words, I'll miss you. I still had it, held between the pages of an Audubon bird guide my dad had once given me.

I went back to my computer and typed in my landlord's name. And there it was. Gaila Crawford. I smiled. At least I'd solved one mystery. Little Gaila must have printed her signature and her secret crush right before they moved. And here it was, all these years later, still proudly proclaiming her mark in this house. I couldn't wait to tell her.

It also put my redecorating plans in a crunch. Because there was no way I could paint over that.

Problems, problems, always problems. I decided to sort it out with a rousing game of *Let's read a good book.* Like Scarlett from Gone with the Wind used to say, "I'll think about that tomorrow."

# CHAPTER 17

After the flurry of activity in the days prior, it was disappointing to see zero appointments on my schedule to see the house.

For something to do, I followed Kari around on a few of her showings. It was always good to get more experience, and her clients were a super nice young couple looking for their first house. They had an adorable baby.

I soon learned that house-hunting with a baby was an adventure on its own. The baby cried, needed to be fed, changed and soothed at almost every stop. I don't even know how the parents could concentrate on the anything that Kari showed them. It made me think I was a long, long, long ways away from wanting a family of my own.

Kari handled it like a pro, even carrying the baby for them at one point. She was patient to the ninth degree and comforted the parents whose nerves were frazzled. I noticed, with the time crunch caused by the baby, that Kari focused on the kitchen and where the baby's bedroom would be located in relation to the parents. She'd take us out to the backyard and say. "Can you just see your kids playing here?"

I thought the showings were going well, but the couple wasn't ready to make an offer. So, they went their way and Kari dropped me off at the office before heading to the school to pick up her kids.

The Flamingo Realty was quiet. Uncle Chris wasn't in, and my email was empty of messages. I felt like I was never going to get the Johnson Lake house sold.

I decided I needed to get out and walk around the town. Take some time to unwind and regroup. Maybe I could think of a new way to advertise the place.

I walked up the street, hands shoved into my pockets and face buried into the front of my coat. The air was crisp and reminded me of the time I'd made apple cider with a friend. I'd arrived to see this metal contraption that looked like an ancient torture device and immediately wondered what the heck I'd gotten myself into. But my friend had squealed and ran over to it, acting like it was the next best thing to chocolate sundaes.

There was a whole crew of us, and we sent what felt like a million apples through it. I ended up sticky, with frozen fingers and cheeks that hurt from laughing so hard. And after one of the guys poured me a glass from a jug that had just been pressed, I understood the excitement. I'd never tasted anything even close to it. It was like Autumn leaves, Halloween, and the first snow had all been bottled together.

I could use some of that now. It also reminded me that I liked people, something I was inclined to forget in my introvertness. I needed to get out and make some friends.

Speaking of people, the sidewalk was busy this afternoon. I had to weave a little bit not to bump into anyone. I couldn't help a smile when I noticed one man ahead of me who looked like he had toilet paper stuck to his shoe.

He strode ahead and the paper did eventually become loose before I'd decided what to do. As I got closer, I noticed it wasn't toilet paper, but a long scroll instead. I glanced toward the building that he'd just exited.

It was the barber shop.

The building's front was green with a full barber pole in the front, twirling red-and-white. I was charmed, to be honest, having not seen one outside of the movies.

As I walked closer, I caught a spicy after-shave scent. I closed my eyes and breathed in deeply. I'd smelled it before.

There was a soda machine out at the store front. The Dr. Pepper button glowed red to warn it was empty. I touched the button, thinking about my Grandpa losing his game of checkers, and then yanked open the barber shop's front door.

A wall of testosterone-laced stares met mine. The vibe was definitely not welcoming.

"Can I help you?" the barber asked. In a twist of irony, he was as bald as a cue ball. He did have an impressive beard that fluffed over his white shirt. He also had a straight razor in his hand with a scary gleam in his eye that said that he was comfortable using it.

The man in the chair before him was hidden under a white mask of shaving cream. One pink stripe shone out from his cheek from the razor's first swathe.

Sitting in one of the chairs waiting for his turn was a young man. He looked vaguely familiar. He had a small cut near his ear, and I wondered if maybe the barber had given him too close of a shave.

"Uh," I started, suddenly drawing a blank. There was another man waiting in a chair. His hair was damp and he stared me down in the mirror with steely blue eyes. What caught my interest was a piece of paper curled around his neck. It protected the collar of his white button-down shirt.

Interesting.

"Would it be too much to ask for a piece of that?" I gestured toward the neck paper.

The barber glanced at it and then back at me incredulously. "You want—"

"Yes, just a short piece. I'm doing a news article." I bluffed like no one's business. For some reason, the phrase "news article" always seemed to grease the wheels of an otherwise awkward conversation.

He shrugged and opened the cabinet behind him, quickly tearing off a section from a box under there. This he handed to me.

"So," I cleared my throat and smiled at the sitting men. "I'm guessing you get a lot of regulars here."

The barber eyed me, and I could nearly see the wheels spinning as he wondered what type of article I was writing. "Sure, of course we do."

"I've been coming for over twenty years. Since Young Sam first opened up." said an old gaffer from one of the chairs. He pointed to the barber and I smiled, realizing "Young Sam," referred to the barber, who was clearly middle aged.

Behind the old man, the wall was covered in plaques and pictures of men in military uniforms. One soldier was heavily decorated in medals.

The old man continued, "And then there's Steve, Roy and Bob,"

My ears perked at the name of Roy, wondering if it was Johnson's property neighbor.

"Don't forget Old Man Lenny," another retiree chimed in.

The mood immediately became more somber as gray nodding heads followed that statement.

"I'm sorry to hear about him," I said, my own head bobbing to mimic their solemn nods.

"He was a great guy. Except for when he crashed his car," the wet-haired guy said.

The old man rolled his eyes and crossed his legs. "She doesn't want to hear that story."

I chimed in. "Actually, I'm new here. I'd like to hear more."

"What's it to you?" he asked.

"Well, I'm the realtor out at that place. I'm the one who discovered him."

A hush fell over the barbershop as they tried to digest my words. Then seven voices spoke at once.

"Well, I'll be!"

"Ain't that something!"

"You the Flamingo's girl? That realty guy's a piece of work."

The old man asked, "You don't happen to be Oscar O'Neil's kid, are you?"

I was surprised. I'd never been referred to by my grandfather before. "Grandkid, actually. Oscar's my grandpa."

"Well, now." The old man smiled and rested his newspaper folded over his knee. "Your grandpa is quite the guy. A champ at checkers."

"Not with Old Man Lenny though!" A few gentle chuckles echoed around the room.

"You know Oscar?" I asked.

"Know him? He stole twenty bucks from me the other day playing rummy. He lives next to that Bed and Breakfast. They have a game going every Tuesday night."

I made a face. "I'm sorry he stole your money."

He laughed, a creaky wheezing sound. "Nah. He's just a good card player is all. He's a stand-up guy." He cocked his head and studied me. "Now that you mention it, you look a little like him."

"But she works for that clown at the Flamingo Realty," said the retiree.

The first man shushed him, moving his hands. "Now don't be

giving her a hard time. This is Oscar's blood. That means she's stand-up too."

I straightened my shoulders. That meant a lot. I wasn't about to spoil it by mentioning the clown was my uncle and Oscar's own son. It was interesting that they didn't know it. It just showed how drastically Uncle Chris had cut ties to his dad when he moved to this town.

"Sure miss Old Man Lenny though," one of the guys said. He started humming.

Another man joined in, and then the barber paused in his shaving. He tipped his head back and his hand bobbed up and down as if trying to catch the beat. Then, he started to sing.

The first two men stood up and followed the barber's tune by carrying the melody.

After a moment, it became obvious they were missing a person. They seemed to notice it too, because one of them said to the young guy, "Come on. You gotta help us out."

The younger guy shook his head bashfully, keeping an eye on me. They kept harassing him. Finally, he stood, looking like he wished the floor would open and swallow him up and said, "Fine, you got me." He cleared his throat as the barber counted out—one, two, three tap. And then he joined in.

It wavered for a few words but then the four voices blended together. And it sounded nice. The kind of nice that brought to mind those old black-and-white TV shows, and sugary cereals in a mini mixed box pack.

When they finished, I was happy to clap. "Great job!" I cheered.

"We need a new member, now that Old Man Lenny's gone," said the barber, returning to shaving. "I guess, Jay's going to have to step in to take his place."

Jay ducked his head and swept his hand in the air, like "no way."

"Yeah, come on, Jay. Practice is at six on Wednesdays. You know you want to."

He shrugged and blushed and sat down, half-falling into the seat. It was cute to see.

There wasn't much more to say and, since I wasn't getting a haircut, I figured it was a good time to thank them and say goodbye. They were gracious as I left, and the barber hollered that any blood of Oscar's was welcome back for a free haircut any time. I laughed at the thought, wondering if a buzz cut was what he had in mind.

# CHAPTER 18

Even though I knew the barber meant no harm, I did take a surreptitious glimpse at my reflection in the next store's window to check out my hair. I hadn't been fussing with it much since my last haircut. I touched the ends and considered a trim when my gaze landed on a beautiful little jar of sea shells in the window sill. I glanced at the name of the store, Second-Hand Treasures, and went inside.

Ten minutes, a jar of shells and a new frying pan later, I left the store. I was getting hungry, so I ordered a sandwich at the Springfield Diner. Marla Springfield was working, so of course I had to say hi. Eighty years old and still cooking for her restaurant.

Sandwich in hand, I headed back. As I passed the barbershop again, several of the men waved. I waved, too and walked with a little extra pep to my step. It was nice to feel like one of the gang.

I opened the door to the office and took a bite of the sandwich as I hurried over to my desk. Uncle Chris had given me a spot behind a series of file cabinets, but it was my space and I loved it. Kari had tried to make it welcoming with a little fern on my desk and Uncle Chris gave me a tiny pink flamingo that bobbed at the slightest vibration. I touched the flamingo now and smiled.

*Okay, down to business.* I was positive the paper I'd found in the Johnson Lake house had come from the barber shop. The aftershave scent was even the same. I'm not sure how the paper got into the house, though. It could have been from Lenny himself, since that was a place he liked to hang out.

But that didn't explain the swim fins. I knew Lenny's were still on his feet when the police dragged him out of the water.

I chewed and thought, frustrated that I still wasn't getting anywhere. I thought about the pendant. I was sure the police had experts investigating that as well, but would I ever get access to what they learned?

Maybe I was on the wrong track assuming it was some sort of jewelry. I remembered the wall of pictures of military men decorated in ribbons and medals. Was it possible it was a medal of some type?

I opened the picture again of the pendant. Honestly, I was impressed the divers found it, being it was so tarnished. I'd probably passed it myself on the shore several times, thinking it was just an odd wet rock.

I clicked my editing settings and messed with the color, contrast, and brightness, trying to see if I could get anything identifying to stand out. What was that? It looked like writing around the circumference, along with the profile of a person's face. I zoomed in more. Bit by bit, some of the letters were becoming distinguishable.

Distinguishable as in I could make out some shapes. But I couldn't read it worth a hill of beans. In fact, some of the letters appeared backward. Still the writing did look strangely familiar, like a type of calligraphy.

I started to sound it out. Maybe it was from reading Polish but I felt like I could almost understand it.

I hit the contrast some more and then took a huge bite of my sandwich. Chewing, I grabbed a pad of paper. I squinted, trying to read, and scribbled what I saw down. There was a G, an L...maybe a D and an M? Some of the letters were melted together under the tarnish.

*All right, here it goes.* I went to Translate app and typed in all the letters I could find. I had to guess at the rest and changed those to O's. Crossing my fingers, I clicked *translate*, hoping for the best.

Not surprisingly, nothing came up.

Frustrated, I pushed the keyboard away. I flicked the flamingo to make it bob. So close. I could feel it. I was so close.

I stared at the picture of the pendant again, but still wasn't coming up with anything different. Finally I typed the letters into the regular search engine bar.

A spelling correction popped up. "Did you mean *Gladium*?"

*Sure, why not.* I clicked it. The search engine brought me back to Translate app, which identified the word as Latin.

Yes! Now I was getting somewhere!

I slammed the key in my eagerness for the English definition. Immediately, it came up. Chills crawled along my arms as I read it.

The explanation said, sword.

*This was it. This has to be it!*

My breath caught in my throat as I went back to the first search bar and typed in the word.

The search engine corrected it with this question, "Did you mean *Gladium meum in Dei obsequium*?"

*Why, yes! Of course! That's exactly what I meant! You must have read my mind.* I copied the phrase and brought it over to the translate box. My hands were shaking.

The definition came up as this, "My sword in the service of God."

My jaw dropped. I pushed back from the desk and stared across to where I could just see Uncle Chris's arm in his office. I had to tell him. This was a huge clue to whatever had been in the house.

Wait, there had to be more. The gamers knew about this. Where had they learned it from? I pasted the phrase in the search bar. All this going back and forth was driving me nuts, but at least I was finally making progress.

The phrase brought up a page of links. I clicked on a couple. They seemed to be for Larpers and people who role-played with swords.

A few links down in the list brought something interesting. It was a news article on some obscure Catholic news site. I clicked on it.

*An old tale of a secret sword has been passed down about a brotherhood of Monks, known as the fighting monks, who defended the small town of Magda when it came under attack from bandits. Dressed only in cloaks, the brothers managed to drive away the bandits with a single sword, before returning peacefully to their monastery.*

*It's interesting to note that the monks were under a vow of silence and neither confirmed nor denied the victory. There was however, a sword found with a medallion stamped on the hilt, that said simply, My sword in the service of God.*

*It was rumored to have been found by a family who later immigrated to America. The sword is famous among period-piece actors, as well as many games. At this date, the monastery is still abandoned.*

I squealed and bounced in my seat. I couldn't believe it! I'd actually done it, dug out a real clue! Whoever found the sword must have immigrated here to this tiny town, bringing the sword. There was no way to know if it was one of Old Man Lenny's relatives, or if they acquired it some other way. But I was completely convinced that was what was found.

It was possible that, during the struggle, the medallion was knocked loose and fell out on the shore.

I could hear Uncle Chris's booming voice on the phone. He sounded angry. I didn't want to disturb him, so I emailed him the web address to the story, along with an explanation of my hypothesis.

Grinning, I took another bite of my sandwich as the warm

glow of satisfaction rolled over me. I couldn't wait to hear what the police thought. *Detective Stella at your service!*

I was about to turn the computer off when, out of curiosity, I decided to check the gamer's forum, Trek's World. I was surprised to see a red thumbs-up at the bottom of the page. Well, that's something. That meant I must have a new message. Telling myself it was probably just a welcome from the moderators, I clicked the notification.

It was from GettingStamped.

**—Hey, where in the world are you, CarmenS? LOL nice name. Couldn't resist. So you heard about the lake? Pretty incredible huh?**

I was surprised by the chatty nature of his message. Maybe this was a good sign. I clicked "reply," and wrote quickly—**It's amazing! Do you think the sword is at the bottom of it?**

I hit send and was about to click off when I noticed three floating dots.

He was typing back.

# CHAPTER 19

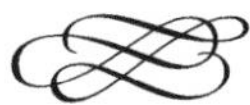

I didn't realize I was holding my breath until his message appeared. A giant gust of air left me as I read—**Ever since I heard about that book by Ava Summers, I've been excited.**

I rubbed my hands together. *Okay, don't blow it. He's on the hook.* I reeled in the line gently with my answer—**You think it really is a sword?**

*Come little fishy, fishy. Tell me your secrets.*

It took him a minute to type, but it finally appeared. —**Yeah, I know it is. And it might already be found. But don't tell anyone I said that, lol.**

He knows it is. His confidence shook my good mood. It felt

ominous. Could this be...was it him that day who dove with Lenny?

My hands were shaking as I typed. —**I wonder if anyone will find it.**

He said,—**Those divers were just stupid. They find a tiny piece of tin, but can't find the sword with obvious directions from Ava Summers' poem.**

I glanced at the last bite of my sandwich, but my nerves were shot and my mouth too dry. I answered,—**It's probably worth millions of dollars.**

He said,—**Something that priceless should be treasured and never sold. You want to grab a cup of coffee and talk about it?**

I covered my mouth. His question freaked me out. The tone he used...did he know me? I mean, was this someone I'd shown the house to the other day? One of those young men?

But how could he? My name, CarmenS, was anonymous.

Then again, how could he assume I lived close enough to him to physically grab a cup of coffee together?

Cold chills ran down my neck and I was shaking my head. *Oh, no, no, no, no. And why did I pick a female user name? Gah!*

I blew out a breath. *Calm down. Maybe he's just fishing, himself.* I pushed up my creative sleeve and responded back. **—My boyfriend wouldn't like that. Sorry**

So I lied. It was one of those things you had to do sometimes to get out of a situation as cleanly as possible. And my red flags were telling me to get out, now.

He answered**—I've heard that one before. LOL It's cool.**

With that, I decided to detach before I got in any deeper. I quickly logged out of Trek's World, wondering how such a great idea turned into such a bad idea so fast.

It was quiet in the Realty. Perfect timing. I headed for Uncle Chris office and tapped on the open door.

"Knock, knock," I said.

"Come in. Perfect timing!"

I laughed at how he used the exact words I was just thinking. We must be family after all.

"What's up?" I asked.

"I just got off the phone with Detective Grayson. I forwarded the link and email you sent me to him. He was actually very impressed with your deductions on the pendant find."

I grinned. "Was he now?"

"Apparently, they'd already come up with the same thing. But, you're work confirmed it. He told me you might be in the wrong profession, and maybe you should consider the police academy."

I shook my head. "I don't think I can handle it. I nearly just got myself a stalker."

"What's this?"

I filled him in on GettingStamped and our conversation.

He rolled his eyes. "Good grief. Just what I need, you getting into some weird trouble out here. Your dad would kill me."

"Don't worry. I cooled him off," I said. "Was there anything else the detective said? Any new leads on the murderer?"

"Nope."

"And Roy..."

"Roy Merlock has a solid alibi. He was out of town that morning getting a delivery of ski supplies, and the supplier confirmed it. Unfortunately, he's clean."

"Well, that's just great," I said glumly.

"The police are guessing it could have been a random person. After the news came out on the internet about the clue and the sword, Old Man Lenny might have just been a victim of being at the wrong place at the wrong time."

"What about the swim fins I found in the house?" I asked.

"I'm not sure. Maybe they were the original owners'."

"They packed everything but their flippers?" I shot back, incredulous.

"Yeah. Maybe." He shrugged and grabbed his *World's Best Boss* coffee mug and took a swig. He burped after that, and I wondered then if there wasn't something stronger than coffee in there. "Anyway, the police are on it."

"I don't know. None of this sits right with me." I frowned.

"Well, you're an analyzer, just like your dad. He always wanted to dig for a deeper reason. But, sometimes the simplest answers are the correct ones."

I shrugged.

"So, do you have plans tonight?" he asked.

"Yeah," I sighed. "I was thinking about some house projects. I have about six gallons of paint in the garage I can use. Might be therapeutic."

"Sounds good. I'll let you know if I hear any more news. Otherwise, I'll see you tomorrow."

I said goodbye and grabbed my jacket from my desk. On my way out, I popped the remaining bit of sandwich in my mouth and refilled my travel mug with some more coffee.

It was colder than earlier outside, and there was a frost in the air. I exhaled a cloud of white. It made me think of me when I'd sit in the back seat of the car as a little girl and draw faces on the window. It drove Dad crazy. So I always drew one angry face with v-shaped eyebrows for him. Naturally, I never told him that.

It was funny how relationships changed after you became an adult. Now that I've had to clean my own car windows a few times, I understood my dad's point of view.

The sky was a dark gray, turning the trees into witchey black shadows with long fingers reaching toward the sky. Kind of a creepy comparison, I realized, but cozy, too. It brought to mind soups and soft scarves and thick socks. It also jogged my memory that I used to have a pair of slippers. I needed to search through my boxes when I got home.

I turned onto my road and pulled next to my mailbox. Of course, I was too far away. I had to do the Stretch-Armstrong reach through the window to be able to snag the mail.

*Oh, what's this?* A nice, fat letter from my dad. There was also a yellow envelope from the mailman requesting additional postage. I read it to find out I owed him twenty-seven more cents. Dad had apparently not added enough stamps.

I couldn't wait to open dad's letter. What a change this move to Pennsylvania had worked in our relationship. It was like he finally respected me as an adult. I loved it.

Maybe I'd save it to open after I cleaned the bathroom. It could be my treat. I ran inside the house to escape the cold and locked the door. After flinging my jacket and purse on the chair, I walked over to the stairwell. Mrs. Crawford's little poem made me smile. I'd forgotten to let her know I'd found it. Taking out my phone, I snapped a picture of the signature, and then forwarded the picture to Mrs. Crawford with the words —**Look at what I uncovered.**

I'd wait to see what she'd say before I made any great decorating plans.

Then, girding up, I cleaned the bathroom, including the dreaded shower stall. Afterward, I made a cup of hot cocoa and went to the living room, bringing my letter.

It was so nice and thick. What had Dad sent me? I couldn't imagine. I slit the envelope and carefully opened it.

It was pictures of me. In one, I was about five, all dressed for my first day of school. Dad had had a heck of a time with my hair. I remember I'd given him a hard time, being terribly picky about the *lumps* and making him redo it several times, but he'd managed to get it in a ponytail.

There was one of the day that he had me help him push the lawn mower. I was in my favorite yellow rubber boots. This one was of me at seven. I was on stage, playing my one-and-only starring role as Goldilocks in the school play. Here was one of me at sixteen as he taught me to change the tire.

There was a short note which said, "Missing my little monkey."

Tears stung my eyes. I sniffed and held the note against my heart. As soon as I could talk, I called him. There was no answer, but I knew he might be busy. He worked crazy hours at the office. I ended my message with I love you and miss you, too.

He was softening. I know he was. I just needed to bide my time until I brought up Grandpa again. But we could be one happy family one day. I knew it in my gut.

Later that night, just before I got ready for bed, I thought about the postage-due envelope. How much did I owe, again? Was there a time limit? I figured I'd better dig the change out now so I could stick it in the box tomorrow.

I got the envelope and squinted to read it. As I looked, a prickle ran down my back. What was *that* mark?

I definitely needed more light to see if I was imagining things.

I hoped to heaven I was.

# CHAPTER 20

I walked into the kitchen, trying to remember where I'd left that scroll of paper I'd found at the Johnson's house. *Where is it?* I lifted the fruit bowl, looked under my purse, opened the junk drawer.

Ah, there it was, hidden with the pens and rubber bands. I smoothed it out and lay the envelope next to it. They both had the same curl under the letter *o*. I suck in my breath. I'd never seen an *o* written that way before. To me that made this a positive match.

Okay, so maybe the mailman did write the note. He could have even written the poem down for Lenny. This doesn't prove anything. At least, not yet.

I sank to the kitchen stool, thinking. Who was the mailman again? Had I ever met him?

Maybe it's a her. I tried to remember, forcing myself to picture a mail truck coming up the road. But he must come when I was at work, because I couldn't think of a time I'd seen him.

This was much too soon after my conversation with GettingStamped, and I was getting tired of getting spooked. *Wait a minute.* Getting stamped, that wasn't a pun on the mail service, was it?

He'd talked like he'd been familiar with me. What was it again? Oh, yeah, he brought up how the diver's had found the pendant, like I'd already mentioned it to him.

I looked back through my messages. I remember talking to him about the lake. But I never said anything about the pendant. How did he know?

Calm down. It's probably because it was in the news.

Then I remembered the news only mentioned the divers weren't able to find anything in the house. GettingStamped had known the real story. He was either there or heavily investigating. That meant he must know who I was, that I was the realtor. There was no other way. That meant I wasn't safe any more.

I rubbed my temples, trying to get a grip. There was something incredibly creepy about talking with a stranger, thinking you were safely-hidden under a mask of anonymity on the internet, only to find out that person knew your identity. Even worse, I didn't know his.

Who was I talking to on Trek's World? Was it actually my mailman? Or was it someone else? Someone who'd been there that day, watching me as I watched the divers? I remember Kari nudging me and pointing out Roy Merlock. That's right...she'd said his son was a mailman. I closed my eyes and grabbed for the counter.

I saw him at the barbershop too. The guy that I'd recognized. He'd sang in the quartet. The roll of paper...it had come from that barbershop.

The barber had mentioned they'd been talking with Lenny about the Johnson Lake and the riddle recently. Had Roy's son been there that day? Seen the interest in Lenny's eyes, maybe even suspected that Lenny was going for one last dive and decided to stalk him?

I was practically hyperventilating. I remembered then that GettingStamped had a Youtube channel. Quickly, I brought it up.

It was the same as the last time I'd searched. I pressed the fast forward, but there was nothing on the video other than a TV screen with a red curtain. I recognized his voice though, now that I'd heard him at the barber shop.

I sat back. Okay, who do I take this crazy idea to? Uncle Chris? Kari? Should I call the deputy directly?

My phone buzzed, making me jump. I fumbled with it, trying to pick it up.

It was a text from Mrs. Crawford.

I laughed at myself. What a reaction! What was I thinking, that GettingStamped had obtained my phone number?

Shaking my head, I clicked it.

She wrote—**I'd forgotten all about that! I was eleven, determined to make my mark and in love with the neighbor boy.**

She was responding to the picture I'd sent of the poem by the stairs. I texted back. **—I was getting ready to paint. Do you want me to save this for posterity?**

She texted back immediately.—**Heavens no. Paint over it.**

Okay. I had my marching orders then.

Her distraction helped me to calm down. That was good. I needed some clear thinking. If it was the mailman, I wasn't going to be a popular person in town. I was barely tolerated since I was related to that 'Flamingo Realty riff-raff.' I didn't think they'd forgive me for getting one of the town's founding father's sons tossed in the pokey.

However, if this founding father's son killed another founding father's descendent, that might change things in their eyes, right? I mean, Old Man Lenny was a chef up at the White Horse restaurant and famous around here. People loved him. You never know, Flamingo Realty might get a boost in the likable department if we found Lenny's killer.

*Sick. Stella. This whole line of thought is sick.*

I shook my head and walked over to the fridge for a box of frozen chicken. *Let me just throw this in the oven and then call Uncle Chris. It'd be good to go over all of this with him. He'll know what to do.*

I was ripping open the box when I noticed a vehicle pull into my driveway.

It was the mailman.

# CHAPTER 21

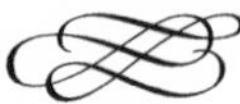

The mail truck drove all the way down the driveway. I didn't stay by the window to watch him park. Instead, I darted to the front door to make sure it was locked. And then I called Uncle Chris.

He answered on the third ring.

"Uncle Chris," I hissed in the phone. Ducking out of sight from the window in the door, I scurried around the corner.

"Stella? What's wrong?"

"Come quick. Call the cops for me."

Well, if that wasn't a shocker, I don't know what one was. Uncle Chris handled it like a champ, probably from years of having his adrenaline worn out on the race course.

"Where are you?" he asked.

"At my house. Remember that guy I told you about? I think he's here stalking me."

"I'm on my way. Don't hang up. Kari! Come quick" Uncle Chris yelled to Kari. She must be in the office as well. "Call 911 and send them to Stella's house. Someone's trying to break in."

That wasn't exactly what was happening, but it could be at any minute.

I crawled along the worn carpet like an inchworm and contorted myself next to the couch so I could peek through the bay window.

The mail truck had parked and someone inside was staring at the house. What was he thinking? Then he looked down for a moment.

Suddenly, my phone dinged. I glanced and saw I had a text from an unknown number.

Package delivery for Stella O'Neil from Steve O'Neil.

That was my father. I peeked out the window. Oh crap! It was the young guy from the barber shop! He was getting out of the truck with what looked like a box in his hands. He also had one of those tablets that you signed when you received something.

I sank down against the wall, thinking hard. Was it possible that my dad had sent something? Was this all a coincidence and I was overreacting?

One thing was for sure, I didn't have to decide what to do. I already knew. Coincidence or not, I was staying here on the floor until he left. I'd seen enough movies to know what happens when the girl second-guesses herself and then dives head first into danger. If it was a legitimate delivery, the package would be waiting for me at the post office.

He stomped up the porch steps, one of the scariest sounds I'd ever heard. I waited on the floor, holding my breath.

"Stella?" Uncle Chris boomed in my ear.

"Shh," I said. "He's here."

"Don't you move, Stella, I'm almost there."

I didn't respond. The door rattled with a knock. My mind was spinning like a top, and I searched around wildly for a weapon. What if he broke in? Where would I go to escape?

One thought froze out all the others. *Oh, no.* Was the back door locked? I glanced at the window. Not seeing him, I army-crawled across the floor to the kitchen. My heart hammered double-time when I realized I didn't hear anything more from the front porch. Was he still there? Or was he trekking around the house, searching for a way in?

I reached the back door, cursing all the windows in the kitchen. Not a single one of them had a curtain. If he walked by, he'd surely see me laying on the floor, flopping about like a seal out of water. *Never mind, just check the door.*

It was unlocked. I bolted it. Still no noise from the front porch. I slowly slid up against the wall until standing. There was the knife block next to the stove. I snatched a knife and held it by my side. My hand trembled.

This little house was smack-dab out in the middle of nowhere. There weren't any close neighbors for me to yell for help. I needed to calm down and think about my options should he break in.

It was hard to focus past the fear. Half of me couldn't believe I was in this situation. I glanced out the kitchen window. *If he comes back here, I'll run for my car. I need to get my keys.*

I dropped back to the floor and began to crawl toward the chair where I'd dropped them when I first came in. There was another knock on the door. I nearly squealed at its unexpected sound.

*Quiet, be very quiet.* I had to cross the front of the hall again. I peeked around the corner, just in time to see him squinting through the door window. I pulled my head back. My face heated from the rush of blood.

*I don't think he saw me. Not down here.*

He disappeared again, and I heard more stomping on the stairs. I waited, trying to listen above my blood pounding in my ears.

Had he really left? Was he trying to fake me out? I peeked again and, seeing no one, I hurried into the living room.

I listened some more, hoping against all else to hear his truck start up.

Nothing.

I army-crawled over to the chair and strained to lift my purse down. It fell and I caught it but wasn't able to prevent it from jingling. I held my breath and waited.

Still nothing.

Carefully, I got out my keys and set the purse down. I needed to get out sight from all these windows. But where?

I finally decided to hide back by the sofa. If I curled right next to it, the sofa shielded me from the bay window, and I could still make it to the front door if I had to run.

Then, I did hear it. Tires crunching down the dirt driveway. Was it him or Uncle Chris? I waited a moment to see what would happen, then peered out the window again.

The mail truck was gone. He had left.

I sank back to the floor, my insides fluttering with a weird mixture of relief and fear. Then I realized the police were on their way. How was I going to explain this?

I realized then I still had my phone squeezed tight in my hand. Uncle Chris had taken me literally, when I'd said Shh. He hadn't made another sound.

"Um, hi," I said, lifting the phone to my ear. "He just left."

"He's gone?"

"Yeah," I laid the knife down on the floor and then covered my eyes. My hands trembled.

"You okay?"

"Yeah. I feel sort of silly. But wait until I tell you my reasons for freaking out."

"I'm here now," he said brusquely.

I sprang up and saw my Uncle's sports car pulling into the driveway. Maybe the mailman had heard a vehicle coming down the road and that's why he left. Maybe he wasn't so innocent after all.

I ran to the door and yanked it open. There was a package on front stoop.

# CHAPTER 22

Welcome to Grand Central. That was my life for the next hour and forty-five minutes. It turns out, when you call about a stalker breaking into a house, more than one cop car shows up. In fact, I had a flood of cop cars, filling the driveway and even parked on the road.

I thought they would all be skeptical about my suspicions of the mailman, what with an actual package being left on the doorstep. But instead, they were a captivated audience. With leather gloves, they took my postage envelope, the paper scroll, as well as screen shots of all my communications with GettingStamped. All my evidence was only circumstantial at this point. But it was enough for one of the Detectives to get a search warrant.

My mailman was indeed Jay Merlock. He must have gotten a

whiff that it was coming because he never showed up back at the post office. I had a feeling passing the parade of cop cars headed my way was the influence behind his disappearance. No one had any idea where he was. That made me uneasy to the ninth degree.

It freaked me out even more when I heard what the police found in his house. He shared it with his father, Roy Merlock, and true to stereotype, Jay lived in the basement.

Apparently, the basement was filled with medieval armor and weapons. Seeing it, I could understand why he was so passionate to add the sword to his collection. I remember him saying that something that priceless should never be sold.

Still, this could have all been chalked up to someone with eclectic interests except for one thing. Found in the corner, under a crocheted brown-and-white zig-zagged blanket, were scuba tanks and face mask. Forensics found DNA as well, caught in the metal hinge of the strap on the face mask. By some amazing stroke of luck, Old Man Lenny must have struck a blow in their fight and grappled with the mask. Forensics came back with it being a positive match for Lenny.

I remembered seeing Jay at the barber shop, and jokingly thinking maybe the barber had given him too close of a shave. He'd had a small cut near his ear. It was chilling to think of now.

As far as what happened on that fateful day, the theory was that Jay had been with Lenny at the barber shop when news of the book being found broke. Jay suspected Lenny would give one more search, especially knowing the owners were gone and the house was up for sale. He also suspected that Lenny would have the best idea where to look, given that it'd been his family's house.

Jay had broken into the Johnson cabin and waited for Lenny to show up. When Lenny entered the lake, Jay followed soon behind him. It was after Lenny recovered the sword, that Jay murdered Lenny.

The medallion fell out of the sword when Jay brought it out of the lake. He may have even gone back to the house to wash up. My arrival to show the house to potential buyers may have caught him by surprise. He hid his flippers—perhaps thinking he didn't want to be caught with them when Lenny was discovered—and disappeared, most likely as I was getting out of the car.

Later, I'd actually seen him, when he'd ostensibly drove up to put a flyer in the mailbox, but really was there to watch.

The murderer always returns to the scene of the crime.

I rubbed my arms, thinking of how close we came to passing one other. While I was admiring the beautiful autumn leaves, he was making his escape. Creepy.

Anyway, everything was ready to be buttoned up and the case solved. There was just one problem.

No one knew where either Jay Merlock or the sword were.

But I had an idea where both could possibly be. I remembered from the videos that there was a red room with a giant tv, a space that wasn't found in the Merlock's house.

I'd shared the channel with the detectives. "Find this room and you'll find him." I was assured that they were searching.

After that there was only one thing left for me to do. It was something more terrifying then anything I'd gone through up to this point.

Tell my dad.

# CHAPTER 23

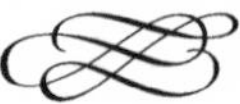

It was somewhere between the removal of the wallpaper in the living room, and the painting of the second wall that I finally worked up my courage to make the call.

Honestly, I don't remember how it went. After he said hello, I blurted out the story in verbal vomit. It wasn't pretty, and at the end, all I could do was hold my breath and brace for his response.

What he said shocked me. "Stella, I'm glad you're safe. You're an adult. I trust you."

My mouth dropped. "Really? You're okay with everything?"

He sighed in the heavy way he used to when I'd try to explain a bad grade on a homework assignment. I cringed and tightened my stomach muscles.

"No, I'm not okay with it. You'll always be my little girl. I dragged it out probably longer than most parents since you're my only child. But you've been taking care of yourself for a few years now. I have to let go." He paused and then added, "Even if I hate it."

I laughed.

"Did you get my package?" he asked.

I did. This time, he'd sent my old childhood stuffed animal, BunBun to me, along with a few books I'd loved growing up. Funny, how much that animal made me smile when I took her out of the box. I may have hugged her for comfort one more time.

Our conversation ended with me getting a promise out of him that he'd think about coming to Pennsylvania to visit. "But I'd rather you come back here. I'll pay for a ticket any time you want," he'd insisted.

So, I was humming as I continued to roll paint on the walls. The color was a light yellow cream, the exact shade of the center of an apple blossom. Already the place was feeling fresh.

I'd even figured out what to do with the poem and signature

at the bottom of the stairs. I couldn't bear to paint over it, so I found a little stencil, and painted green leaves around it like a frame. I couldn't wait to show Mrs. Carmichael.

Later that night, after a long bath, I climbed on the bed with my great-great Grandma's letters. I smoothed a new one out and opened up the Translate app on my phone. But the sight of the app honestly gave me anxiety, remembering how I'd used it to translate the sword poem. I tucked everything away again. I'd try in the daylight, when Translate didn't make me immediately think of the mailman on my front porch.

Instead, I wandered downstairs and found my jar of seashells, my treasure from the second-hand store. I carefully spilled them across the kitchen table.

They were so pretty. The pale blues and mother-of-pearl iridescent insides made me want to lick it. What an odd feeling, but I did give it a tiny lick. Salty.

It was then I realized what had attracted me to them. I'd collected some shells similar to these when I was a little girl. I think it was my first time Dad had taken me to the ocean.

The ocean had been a monster that day, pounding the shore, roaring, and leaving behind slimy trails of green. I'd been terrified and wouldn't leave the piles of driftwood to go down to the beach.

Dad had been patient. He'd offered to carry me, but I'd

shaken my head, too terrified. Finally, he sat on one of the logs and patted the empty space next to him.

"Let's listen," he said. "The waves are telling a story."

After hesitating a bit, my fingers in my mouth, I sat next to him. And we'd listened. Soon, I caught the rhythm of the waves. The roar, the splash and the shhh as it gathered itself back to hit the shore again.

"What's it saying, Stella?" Dad asked.

"It's saying it likes to eat little girls," I answered.

Dad drew in the sand with a stick. I saw that what he drew was a tiger, my favorite animal at the time. "Tigers can be dangerous as well, but we can see them at the zoo, right?"

I nodded.

"And why is that?"

"Because they have fences around them."

He nodded. "That's right. And oceans have fences around them as well. They only come up so far, and then they go back. And every night and every day they come to the edge of their fence to peek at the world. But they like their space. You see, they take care of the fish, and the whales, and the dolphins. And even the tiny crabs and animals that live in seashells."

And then he smiled at me, his eyes sparkling. "Do you know that crabs carry their homes on their back?"

I shook my head, and my fingers went back to my mouth. This time I noticed they tasted salty.

"They do. And wherever they go, their home goes with them." He put his arm around me. "Did you know that we are like crabs?"

"I don't have a shell." I giggled.

He smiled too. "That's true. But wherever we go, as long as we are together, we always have a home." He squeezed me tight. "Now, would you like to go down and see if we can find any abandoned seashells?"

I stared at the water again. Dad said it was like a tiger. It wouldn't leave its fence. "Will the crabs need their shells?"

"Not these, Sweet Pea. These are the jewels the sea gives us for free."

We'd gone down together, my hand in his. And when I left, my pockets were bulging with shells.

I turned the shell over in my fingers, smiling at the sweet memory, a little puzzle piece that reminded me of who I was and what mattered most to me.

As I thought of Dad, my phone dinged with a text. I reached

for it in surprised, wondering if somehow it was from him and he knew I was thinking about him.

It was from Uncle Chris. Relief filled me like I was taking my first deep breath in a long time. He wrote —**They got him. Turns out the room was inside a cargo container out on their property. Found the sword too. And get this. A full-price offer came through for you to review in the morning on the Johnson house. From a couple represented by Angela Cranton. Good job, my number one Flamingo Realtor!**

I grinned nearly ear-to-ear. This was the best news ever.

I was getting my hot rod after all.

# CHAPTER 24

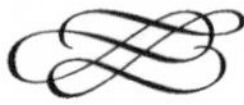

There was one more small thing that happened after all of this. I guess you could call it an epilogue to my crazy week.

Uncle Chris called me late Friday evening. His voice was slurred and he sounded like he'd tipped more than a few back.

"Stella," he said, gruffly.

"Yes, Uncle Chris." I shook my head, humoring him.

"I'm sorry for calling so late."

I realized then that he was nervous. "You're fine. What's up?"

"I...I've had something on my mind ever since that one conversation we had."

"What conversation?"

He took a deep breath and I could practically hear his nostrils flare as he gustily exhaled. "The one at Darcy's. You know, where you asked if I'd ever find someone?"

Oh, my gosh. This was it. Finally, an O'Neil was about to crack in regards to one of their secrets. I gripped the phone and nodded before realizing he couldn't see me. "Yeah, I remember."

"I didn't want to say anything, not with Kari there. It's..." he paused as if suddenly lost for words.

"You don't have to say anything. I'm actually sorry I pried," I said, feeling horrible I'd caused him all this angst.

"No, it's not that. But it's something I need to talk to you about—uh—face to face. Are you going to be around tomorrow?"

What on earth was the big secret? "Yeah, I think so."

"Okay, how about we meet at Darcy's again?"

"Sure. I can do that."

"I'll text you the time." He sighed again. "The only thing is, Stella, I don't want you to be mad at me."

And with that, he hung up, leaving me to stare at the phone in wonder.

The End

Thank you for reading A Dead Market. The story continues! Check out book three in Flamingo Realty, Home Strange Home.

Here are a few more series to whet your appetite.

Baker Street Mysteries— join Georgie, amateur sleuth and historical tour guide on her spooky, crazy adventures. As a fun bonus there's free recipes included!

Cherry Pie or Die

Cookies and Scream

Crème Brûlée or Slay

Drizzle of Death

Slash in the Pan

Oceanside Hotel Cozy Mysteries—Maisie runs a 5 star hotel and thought she'd seen everything. Little did she know. From haunted pirate tales to Hollywood red carpet events, she has a lot to keep her busy.

Booked For Murder

Deadly Reservation

Final Check Out

Fatal Vacancy

Suite Casualty

Angel Lake Cozy Mysteries—Elise comes home to her home town to lick her wounds after a nasty divorce. Together, with her best friend Lavina, they cook up some crazy mysteries.

The Sweet Taste of Murder

The Bitter Taste of Betrayal

The Sour Taste of Suspicion

The Honeyed Taste of Deception

The Tempting Taste of Danger

The Frosty Taste of Scandal

And here is Circus Cozy Mysteries— Meet Trixie, the World's Smallest Lady Godiva. She may be small but she's learning she has a lion's heart.

Cirque de Slay

CEECEE JAMES

Big Top Treachery

Made in the USA
San Bernardino, CA
09 August 2019